"Aidan, you're here."

Emmy was stunned, her tone forming a question mark. Somehow she'd never expected to see him back at Promise Lake.

Aidan, her college sweetheart—the man her parents had considered a part of the family, before everything went wrong. She'd been too young, too ambitious, too *everything* back then.

He blinked, silent. She hadn't seen him in person in well over a decade. The sight of him, in person after all these years, struck her like a physical blow.

Here was the life she hadn't chosen, standing right before her.

Dear Reader,

This is my first novel for Harlequin Superromance, and I've loved having the chance to explore some diverse issues that are near to my heart—environmentalism, the emotional fallout from war and violence, and the trials of single parenthood.

Aidan Caldwell is perhaps the most scarred character I've ever written, and his journey to healing, I hope, serves as a tribute to everyone who faces a difficult time after a traumatic event.

And as a single parent, I know well the challenges of balancing parenthood with other demands. With Emmy and Max, I enjoyed the chance to create a mother-child relationship in all its unglamorous glory.

Finally, I am passionate about sustainable architecture, so it was only natural to have my architect heroine building a house that leaves a light footprint on the earth. Small houses, green building practices and modern prefab are all topics I like to discuss, so please feel free to e-mail me if you'd like to know more.

I also love hearing from readers, period. You can reach me at jamiesobrato@yahoo.com, and you can learn more about me and my upcoming books at www.jamiesobrato.com.

Sincerely,

Jamie Sobrato

A FOREVER FAMILY
Jamie Sobrato

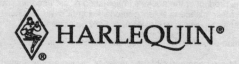

HARLEQUIN®

TORONTO • NEW YORK • LONDON
AMSTERDAM • PARIS • SYDNEY • HAMBURG
STOCKHOLM • ATHENS • TOKYO • MILAN • MADRID
PRAGUE • WARSAW • BUDAPEST • AUCKLAND

Recycling programs
for this product may
not exist in your area.

ISBN-13: 978-0-373-71536-7
ISBN-10:   0-373-71536-6

A FOREVER FAMILY

www.eHarlequin.com

Printed in U.S.A.

ABOUT THE AUTHOR

Jamie Sobrato has always wanted to be a writer, though unlike the hero in this novel she never has trouble with her books being hundreds of pages too long. She writes for Harlequin Superromance and Harlequin Blaze, and she lives in a small Northern California town with her two children, two rabbits, two lizards and one snake. Her hobbies include hiking, reading and sleeping.

Books by Jamie Sobrato

HARLEQUIN BLAZE

237—ONCE UPON A SEDUCTION
266—THE SEX QUOTIENT
284—A WHISPER OF WANTING
316—SEX AS A SECOND LANGUAGE
328—CALL ME WICKED
357—SEX BOMB
420—SEDUCING A S.E.A.L.

To Alexander Sobrato,
who carries my heart wherever he goes

PROLOGUE

August 21, 1947
Promise Lake, California

LETICIA VAN AMSTED would die with dirt beneath her fingernails. She sat on the beach next to the lake and stared at her pale, thin hands marred by half-moons of soil at each tip, and she thought it ironic that after a lifetime of caring so much for her hands, this was how they looked on the last day of her life.

But she'd needed to bury her secrets, and bury them she had. She did not want her family sorting through her belongings later, shaking their heads at her foolishness, tut-tutting over the most intimate details of her life.

And yet, she could not destroy those secrets, either. She could not make herself burn the things she held dearest in life, the evidence of the love that had consumed her and destroyed her, so she buried it all instead.

By the time anyone found those secrets, she would be long gone, but at least they would understand that her possessions were cherished. They were things to be held dear.

The sun had almost set behind the hills on the west

side of the lake. She watched the light fade from gold to shadow, and when it turned from shadow to blackness, she would say good-night to this earth one last time. Her heart was too broken to do anything else.

She was too ashamed to let the world know she was ending her own life, so she would swim out into the lake, and her family would believe she'd drowned when they found her body. She would swim until she was exhausted, and then she would let the water take away this pain that made going on too much of an effort to bear.

She could think of no better place to live than on the verdant shores of Promise Lake, and she could think of no better place to die than in its deep, cold, cleansing water.

CHAPTER ONE

I am haunted by the image of a woman I saw
running from the militia, a baby in one arm and
a small boy gripping her hand. They looked terrified. There is little chance they survived, but I
do not know for sure, because they were the last
people I saw before my capture, the final vision
of a city destroyed by war and descended into
chaos. Sometimes it's not the sight of violence
and death that is most disturbing, but rather the
moments just before.

From *Through a Soldier's Eyes*
by Aidan Caldwell

Present Day
Promise Lake, California

THIS WAS NOT her fairy-tale ending.

This old Mercedes loaded down with possessions, ar-
tifacts of a scattered life and broken marriage, this weary,
battered pair of travelers, limping toward a new life, they
were no prince and princess riding off into the sunset.

The contrast almost made Emmy Van Amsted laugh. Almost.

She glanced into the rearview mirror at the one happy thing she could point to in her life right now. A round, scruffy head bowed, studying a book about rocks and minerals that Emmy knew from bedtime reading last night contained words she had trouble pronouncing.

When everything else about her life sucked beyond words, she comforted herself again and again with the physical fact of Max.

At the age of thirty-five, she had at least acquired enough wisdom to know her son was a much more precious prize than any Prince Charming. She knew enough now, a year after the end of a very public and very painful divorce, to understand that there were very few helpful truths in fairy tales anyway.

If only life were as simple as evil stepmothers and valiant men on white stallions.

But no, a woman had to make her own happiness, slay her own dragons and ride off into the sunset on her own steed. Exactly what Emmy was doing now. Well, not into the sunset, but rather the soothing comfort of the northern California redwoods and the peaceful silence of Promise Lake, that placid blue body of water in the woods that had haunted her dreams since childhood.

"Mom, can we look up Tibet on the computer again when we get to the cabin?"

Emmy's stomach lurched.

"Sure, soon as we get an Internet connection. We might not have one for a few days, okay?" She suffered a stab of guilt at denying her son even the ability to search for things online right now, when it seemed as though nearly everything about his normal life had been taken away.

"Um, okay," he said.

Maybe she was overreacting a wee bit, she'd realized yesterday when she'd caught herself promising him any toys he wanted once they were settled in their new place.

But if their old life had crumbled, she felt like she might be able to grab on to some real and lasting happiness for them both if she could build a new life here in the midst of so much rubble.

No, not if. *When.* Looking in the rearview mirror at Max reminded her that there was no option of failing now. She owed him—and maybe even herself—a better life than they'd left behind. She could not live with herself if her own failures caused her son permanent scars that wouldn't heal.

"Do you think Daddy has the Internet in Tibet?"

"I doubt it, honey. At least not every day."

As she steered her car onto the gravel road that led to their family's summer house, she willed the anger to drain from her. She was not going to be one of those bitter divorced women who blamed her every problem on her ex. She was going to accept the part her choices had played in leading her to her current destiny, and she was not going to point fingers.

She didn't want to give the selfish bastard that much power over her.

"Does Tibet have Internet cafés like in San Francisco?"

"Yes, I imagine there are some."

"Will Daddy write e-mails to me?"

"I'm sure he will. And he'll call too, okay?"

Except he hadn't in the two weeks since he'd left the U.S. on his spiritual quest.

"Mommy, what's the capital of Tibet?"

"I'm not sure, honey. We'll have to look it up."

Max had been reading since a few months before his fourth birthday, and was, much to the amazement of most of the adults around him, a genius. Sometimes Emmy wished she could take that burden away from her little boy and let him be normal. Let him be possessed of an average imagination rather than an out-of-control one, let him have a level of knowledge that matched his six-year-old emotional development, let him not already be suffering from existential angst the likes of which most adults never faced.

But she could not do that any more than she could undo the past two years of stress and sadness she'd put him through while divorcing his father.

"Can we go looking for rocks when we get to the cabin?"

"Maybe later, honey. We should probably get unpacked and buy some groceries first."

They rounded the curve into the clearing where the house sat at the end of the long gravel drive, and Emmy was surprised to see a black motorcycle parked out front.

Fear filled her belly. Squatters in the cabin? It wasn't unheard of, but as far as she knew it had never happened to anyone on this side of the lake. She parked the car and sat for a few moments, reviewing her options. She could leave, call the sheriff to report an intruder and let them handle the situation. But that seemed kind of a drastic reaction in a town where the most dangerous thing that ever happened was people getting drunk and going swimming after dark.

Or she could knock on the door and pretend she was a lost tourist if the person who answered seemed menacing.

She flipped open her cell phone, was relieved to see she had a strong signal, and predialed 911, just in case, so she could hit the call button if necessary.

"Stay in the car, sweetie," she said to Max. "I'm going to lock the door just to be safe while I'm gone."

"But we're in the middle of the woods," he argued logically.

"There might be bears."

"Bears can't open car doors. Hey, whose motorcycle is that?" he said, finally noticing the intruder.

"I don't know. I'm going to go check now."

Emmy braced herself and got out.

She locked the car and marched up the drive, past the spot where she'd fallen at the age of six and cut her knee open on a sharp rock, past the shiny black, unwelcome Harley-Davidson with California plates, and up the wood steps onto the cabin's porch. Her stomach still clenched, she knocked loudly. Her palm holding the cell phone was damp with sweat.

A moment later, she heard footsteps inside, and the door opened. Through the ancient screen door, she saw a man whose face she recognized—a face that brought memories flooding back.

"Aidan?" she said, stunned, her tone forming a question mark.

He blinked, silent. She hadn't seen him in well over a decade. The sight of him, right here in person after all these years, struck her like a physical blow. Here was the life she hadn't chosen, standing right before her.

She swallowed the sick, acidic taste in her mouth and willed herself not to panic.

Aidan, her college sweetheart at Stanford, the man her parents had considered a part of the family before everything went wrong. She'd been too young, too ambitious, too *everything* back then.

And him, he'd been a wild mustang ready to charge out into the world, which is exactly what he'd done after she'd ended their relationship.

Some part of her had been proud of him for moving on, and some other less-rational part had felt a little abandoned, even though she'd been the one doing the breaking up. She'd always thought, back then at least, that he'd be a part of her life in one way or another.

More recently though, she'd seen him on the news— the tragedy of his time as a peacekeeper in Darfur, his capture, the torture, the bloody escape….

Finally, he spoke. "Emmy."

His voice resonated deep inside her, creating a warm humming sensation that she forced herself to ignore.

"What are you doing here?"

"Your father loaned me the cabin," he said.

Her father?

She shouldn't have been surprised. It was as if the man thought up ways to annoy his oldest daughter in his sleep.

"But…my mother told me we could stay here, that it was empty."

This was the problem with a set of divorced parents who still shared a vacation property neither of them much used. Utter and complete lack of communication. Not that she could blame her mother for not speaking to her father. Emmy rarely spoke to the son of a bitch either.

"We? As in your husband?" he said, peering over her shoulder at the car.

"No." He didn't know about her divorce then. Or her child. "My son, Max. He's six."

She flipped her cell phone shut and slipped it into her pocket, figuring she was at least safe from squatters.

His gaze cut back to her. "Oh."

His eyes looked tired, like he'd seen too much, and at the same time, oddly keyed up, like he might bolt at any moment. Still darkly gorgeous as ever, he was only thirty-seven, but he'd lived a lot in those years. He'd always been in the middle of the action, for as long as she'd known him. It hadn't completely surprised her to see his name pop up in media, since he'd spent his entire career in the military working overseas, and he'd gained experience peacekeeping in Bosnia, so it made sense that he might end up in Darfur, too.

"We just drove up from San Francisco. I'm moving here, actually."

His eyebrows shot up. "You? Moving? *Here?*"

"Why is that so hard to believe?" His disbelief stung, not so much because it was misplaced as because it suggested he didn't know the real her anymore. And why should he? Their lives had gone down different paths. They'd both changed in response to their differing terrain.

"Weren't you living on Nob Hill in a mansion with your investment-banker husband?"

He didn't use Steven's name, of course. He probably refused to even speak it aloud.

Emmy felt a surge of anger that she fought to quell. "We're divorced now," she said evenly.

"Oh." He had the grace, at least, not to look smug at the news, which diffused her anger a bit.

"You'll have to excuse my abruptness, but I don't want to talk about all that now. It's really not your business why I'm moving. What matters is that you're living in the house I intend to live in, and you need to vacate."

"Yeah, that's a problem. I guess you'll have to find another place to stay though, because I can't leave," he said, his voice flat.

After a long drive, half of it through heavy traffic as she'd made her way out of the Bay Area, she felt the last of her patience vanish. "I don't remember you being such an asshole," she said.

He looked unimpressed by her anger. "You used not to be a backstabber."

Emmy didn't let him see her reaction. She deserved that one. She shouldn't have let herself fall for his childhood best friend, shouldn't even have considered it, even though Aidan had gone off to serve in the military.

"You know everything's booked for the season up here. I can't just find another place to stay at the drop of a hat."

"Neither can I."

"This is my family's house."

"And I'm your father's guest."

His angry undercurrent had a way of making him seem larger than life. He was already an imposing man, six foot two and solid muscle. Where once he'd been a college kid, now he looked menacing in a way he never had before, and Emmy felt the tiniest hint of fear, because she didn't know him anymore. He'd seen a world of pain and suffering since those carefree days of their youth.

Since it had all fallen apart with Aidan's proposal of marriage and her answer that they were too young, that it would never work, that she wasn't ready. Instead of saying yes to him that night, a few days before graduation, she'd broken up with him.

Emmy, uncharacteristically, felt her throat constrict

with a grief that welled up out of nowhere. She wasn't the type to cry when she didn't get her way. No, she knew how to fight for what she wanted—a skill she'd honed to perfection in the male-dominated architecture world. But maybe this felt too much like her luck lately, too much like one more obstacle she didn't have the energy to overcome.

Something about Aidan's demeanor, brittle and nervous, told Emmy not to push him right now. She willed the grief away and amazed herself by saying, in a firm, steady voice, "I'll stay in the guest cottage out back, until you find another place to live."

It was a temporary solution, but it wouldn't last for long. Maybe when Aidan stopped looking as though he was about to go postal, she could convince him to move to the guest cottage. Or, better yet, maybe her uncomfortable proximity would convince him to vacate the property altogether. Whatever happened, it needed to happen soon, because the one-room cottage would be cramped quarters for Emmy and Max. And if Aidan couldn't see that, then he was just as crazy as that look in his eyes suggested.

NOT EVERY PRISON had bars on the windows. Some didn't look like prisons at all, and some existed only in the mind, but were no less punishing than those constructed of stone and steel.

He still saw their faces. He still heard their cries. That was the worst legacy of the most horrific weeks, days, hours and minutes of his life. The echoes of pain, the memories of inhuman cruelty and the gazes of children whose eyes had seen too much.

Aidan woke in a cold sweat in the early, dark hours of the morning, every morning, without fail. And in those lonely moments, he lay awake staring at the walls as if they were the enemy. This was the thing people didn't understand about the angry, empty look in his eyes. They didn't understand that he was still living in this hell they all thought he had escaped so heroically.

There had been no escape.

And the longer he lived here, the more this cabin became a prison of his own making, until lately, the sight of another person was enough to send him cringing into bed, his eyes shut tight, hoping they would go away. Hoping the whole goddamn world would just go away.

And now… This.

Emmy.

Emmy divorced.

Why did the universe continue to torture him in such cruel and unusual ways?

Aidan locked the bathroom door, flicked on the light, and stared at his haggard, unshaven face in the mirror. A week's growth of beard had given him the requisite mountain-man look, and a jagged scar across the left side of his forehead gave him what a few women had kindly called "character."

But all he could see was the haunted wretch he'd become.

He should shave.

No, that would be too obvious, like he was trying to impress Emmy. And he definitely didn't want to impress her. No freaking way.

Brush his hair then? Wash it?

No. He had had it cut eight or nine months ago, and it had grown shaggy, hanging to his collar, if he'd ever bothered to wear a shirt with a collar, rather than the faded black T-shirt that had become part of his new recluse uniform.

A recluse—one thing he'd never imagined himself becoming. He'd once been fully engaged with the world around him. Before his time in Sudan, he'd lived and breathed for human interactions.

His hands were shaking. They did that often at odd times. Usually when he had to talk to people.

And Emmy wasn't just any people. She'd haunted him in her own way for all the years since he'd last seen her. He'd almost not come here, because of the memory of her, because of the summer they'd spent here in college, making love beneath the redwoods and in the cool water of Promise Lake.

That impulse, he saw now, had been a wise one. But her father had been so insistent, and Aidan had needed a place to escape where no one would think to look for him. He'd tried living in the city, tried going about his life as if nothing had changed. But it had all felt like such a huge lie, he couldn't stand it.

Everything had changed. Nothing inside him was the same. He'd had his insides ripped out by what he'd seen, and what had formed inside him after was a new landscape full of horrors and nightmares. He sometimes felt like a child again, like a little boy hiding his head under the covers here in this isolated cabin, trying to pretend the bogeymen under the bed and in the closets weren't really there, hoping they'd leave him alone until morning light chased them away.

Unfortunately, hiding out had a disadvantage. It gave him time to remember all the real horrors. One boy's face in particular. A child, maybe Max's age, standing on the side of a dirt road, a dead, decapitated man at his feet. His father?

Aidan never had a chance to ask as his vehicle rolled past. The boy's eyes were hard, so full of hurt that there was no more room for pain, and his face was permanently seared into Aidan's memory like so many others. They appeared to him at odd times, as he was trying to fall asleep, or as he poured milk into his coffee, and their appearances never stopped feeling like a kick in the gut.

The horrors aside, this cabin had been a suitable hideout from the world for the past six months. People rarely even ventured down the private gravel road that led here, barring the occasional lost tourist.

But Emmy.

Here.

Now.

Divorced.

And with a son.

It seemed too cruel to be true. A whole new kind of horror to face.

Any sane person would have turned tail and run out of a healthy sense of self-preservation, but it wasn't like Aidan could really apply the term *sane* to himself anymore. Lately, even stepping out the back door onto the deck seized him with an anxiety attack. No way could he consider relocating now.

Okay, so he couldn't hide out in the damn bathroom forever. He had to go back out into the rooms with windows and risk spotting Emmy—or the kid—out there in the yard.

This was almost too much to consider.

But it was the lesser evil than hiding out like a coward and having to look at himself in the mirror. He had to get out of this rock-bottom rut and do something different from what he'd been doing. He wanted to get better, not worse.

Hands still shaking, he turned the lock on the door knob, then eased the door open. To the left, the bedroom, from which he could see out to the guest cottage. Or to the right, the living room, which overlooked where their car was parked, the car they were probably unloading now.

Through an open window came a boy's voice calling, "Mommy, look! A red-tailed hawk!"

He froze. His stomach pitched, and he bolted back into the bathroom and lost his lunch in the toilet.

Crouched there on the tile floor a few minutes later, he wiped away the cold sweat on his forehead and said a silent prayer that some miracle might deliver him from this hell.

Then he rinsed his mouth out, turned back to the door, and tried again. This time, he made it all the way into the living room before the sight of Emmy's station wagon as he was drawing the curtains shut became too much to bear, and he had to rush to the bathroom again.

CHAPTER TWO

> There is no one face of war. There are many faces.
> As children playing soldier, we play with guns,
> we play at killing. Then there is reality, which I
> saw up close in Darfur. I saw that the people who
> suffer in war are someone's mother, someone's
> child, someone's husband, someone's brother.
>
> From *Through a Soldier's Eyes*
> by Aidan Caldwell

"THIS IS absurd."

Emmy caught herself clutching the phone as if it was
a life preserver and she was on a sinking ship. She
loosened her grip. On the other end of the line, her
mother was making apologetic noises about how she'd
forgotten to check with Robert about the cabin before
telling Emmy it was empty.

"It'll be good to have a man around there. Maybe
you two will pick up where you—"

"Mother! Don't say it."

"Well, you were quite the thing—"

"Don't. Say. It."

"I don't know why you have to be so dramatic."

Anna Hawthorne had spent her life carefully not being too dramatic about anything. She was east-coast proper, she liked to say, which Emmy knew was code for "well-bred in a way these Californians I foolishly married into are not."

It was a tribute to Anna's cheery sense of martyrdom that she had not packed up and gone back to Boston after her own divorce. That, and she couldn't bear to be so far from her children and grandchildren.

"I'm not here to find a husband," Emmy said, leaving out the part about not ever intending to marry again.

Ever, ever, ever.

The pain of going through divorce—especially with a small child—was too staggering, the havoc wreaked on their lives too devastating, to go through it again. And the only way to avoid divorce, as far as Emmy could tell, was to avoid marriage.

"In my day, a single woman was happy to find a handsome, eligible man in her life."

"I just got divorced two years ago. Divorced? Remember that? You went through it once upon a time."

Except, unlike Emmy, Anna had remarried as soon as another man had come along. She hadn't gotten permanently jaded about romance by the loss of her marriage the way Emmy had. At times though, Emmy wasn't sure if the failure of imagination was on her side or her mother's. Something about Anna's eternal optimism made Emmy feel a little like a grouch and a failure.

"Yes, dear. And I'm sorry. I know you're still

carrying around a lot of pain. I was just hoping you could look for the roses instead of the thorns for once."

Emmy bit her tongue. Anna didn't understand her oldest daughter, the most headstrong and driven of all her children, and she never had been able to relate to her the way she could to the younger two.

"I have to go, Mom. Please ask Robert to call Aidan and tell him he'll have to vacate the cabin by next week."

After she hung up the phone and placed it on the little dinette table that occupied one corner of the tiny guest cottage, Emmy stared out the window at the cabin. Okay, so she was a coward.

She couldn't bear to talk to her father since discovering that her own husband was just as much an adulterer as her dad had been. The sound of his voice felt like a betrayal to her now, and accepting him again as a part of her life felt like saying that being a cheater was okay. Her mother might have gotten over his adultery and moved on, but Emmy hadn't.

Not for a second.

She was a coward, but she also saw the wisdom of being kind to herself. She was too emotionally drained to deal with something as complicated as those old wounds right now.

Not only would she not call her own father, but she wouldn't walk across the lawn and discuss the matter with Aidan again like an adult. Not after that last encounter, which had left her filled with that odd grief of unknown origin.

But unfortunately, *coward* was one word no one would ever apply to Max. She watched, her mouth dry, as he crossed the yard and knocked on the back door of the cabin. When no one answered, he simply knocked harder. And after that when no one answered, he tried the doorknob.

Emmy hopped up in horror, reacting in slow motion, and called out his name. "Max! Leave that door alone!"

But he couldn't hear her, and apparently the door was unlocked, because as she hurried to their own door calling out for him to stop, he walked right into the cabin.

AIDAN ONLY realized as he watched the back door open that he'd neglected to lock it. He sat on the bed, willing his hands to stop shaking, as the boy came in and stood in the dusty afternoon light.

"Hi," the kid said.

Aidan didn't answer. He wanted to tell the little carbon copy of Emmy to get the hell out, but even in his current state he had enough decency not to say that to a child.

"I'm Max," the kid said.

Aidan said nothing as the kid stared, unblinking, at him.

"Are you a pirate?"

He'd been called worse things. But still he couldn't produce any words. And the boy was starting to look a little unnerved by the silence.

"You look like a pirate."

"Yeah?" Aidan managed to croak.

"This is my grandma's cabin. Do you know her?"

"Yep."

The boy closed the door, just as his mother was calling his name from outside. And smiling mischievously, he locked it behind himself. Aidan still could not manage to loosen his throat for long enough to tell the kid to get out.

Max crossed the room and got down on his hands and knees in front of the desk. Then he squeezed past the chair and wedged himself beneath the desk. "Shh," he said. "Don't tell my mom I'm under here. I'm a stowaway."

A stowaway? Were kids that little supposed to use words that big? He thought of his own giggling nephews, whom he hadn't seen in months. One of them, Andrew, was about the same size as this kid. Aidan loved those boys fiercely, but he couldn't bring himself to see his family—especially not his nephews—in his current state. He was ashamed of how pathetic he'd become, and there was no way to reconcile his inability to leave the house with the kids' hero worship of him.

Now he only wanted to curl up and pretend the rest of the world wasn't still out there, vulnerable to all that pain and hurt he could never stop from happening.

The boy was peering out at him now. "How come you don't talk much?" he asked.

His face was so innocent, so untouched by the hard truths of life.

Aidan turned away from him. Emmy was knocking on the door, and he knew he would have to answer.

"Max!" she called through the door. "Aidan? Could you please open up? My son is in there."

He dragged himself from the bed and across the room. He unlocked the door and jerked it open. Silently, he pointed to the desk, then turned and left the room without saying a word. He was well aware that he was behaving like a freak, which was exactly why he didn't want people around.

Hands shaking again and a headache beginning to pound at his temples, he slumped on the sofa in the living room and hoped like hell his unwelcome guests would vacate the house without bothering him. But it was a futile hope, because a moment later, the sound of footsteps came down the hallway.

"I'm sorry," Emmy said from the doorway. "Max is used to being able to come and go at will around here. I'll make sure he knows not to come in uninvited again."

Aidan forced his gaze toward her. She was more beautiful than she used to be. The smooth-skinned perfection of youth had given way to something more interesting. She had laugh lines, more prominent cheekbones and a certain knowing quality in her eyes. Her dark-brown hair, that she'd always worn in a thick, glossy braid during college, was a little shorter now, hanging only to the middle of her back, parted on the side and tucked behind her ear.

The sight of her had never failed to stop his heart short and catch his breath in his throat. She'd been his first love. His only true love. Once upon a time, he'd thought they'd be together forever.

But over the years, the love had turned to bitterness, and then to acceptance that she was only a painful chapter of his past.

Until now.

"Are you okay?" she asked when he didn't answer.

He made his head move up and down in something resembling a nod.

But she was still standing there, staring at him.

"Could we at least be civil to each other while we're stuck like this?"

"I need to be left alone," he finally said. "I'm writing a book."

"Oh. Sorry. I mean, that's great. I'm sorry we're bothering you."

And with that, she turned and left. He cursed himself for letting his gaze sweep over her retreating form, the slim torso in a stretchy white tank top and the lush curve of her hips and ass in a pair of faded jeans. He'd gone too long without a woman, and his dick instantly went hard, betraying all his neuroses. He'd always been crazy about Emmy's body. He still could recall the details of her flesh as if it were his own.

He wondered how age and motherhood had changed the parts of her he couldn't see, then he cursed himself for the torturous thought.

Aidan stared at the empty hallway where she had been, listening as she cajoled her son out the back door and shut it behind them. When they were gone, he shot up and checked each door to make sure they were locked. Then, to be safe, he checked all the windows too, shutting and locking the ones he'd had open for the breeze.

By the time he finished, his erection was mercifully gone, but he knew if he let his thoughts stray for long, he'd be tortured all over again.

Memories of Emmy had tormented him less and less over the years, but having her here reminded him of the future he'd lost, the different paths they'd taken.

How the hell was he supposed to work?

Okay, so it was absurd how little his day consisted of anymore. Him, alone at his computer, working on a manuscript that had already gone on two hundred pages too long, with no end in sight. Why had he thought it would be a good idea to write a memoir of his time in Darfur?

Okay, the hefty advance his agent had gotten him had been a big step towards persuading him to do it. But he'd actually believed putting it all on paper would be therapeutic. So far, it had only edged him further and further away from sanity. But the book was his excuse for every eccentricity now. It was his official reason for not going anywhere, or talking to anyone, for having groceries delivered and rarely even answering his e-mail. He didn't answer the phone normally, either, so when it rang just as he was sitting down at the computer, he let the answering machine pick up.

"Say there, Aidan my boy," came a baritone voice he recognized instantly as Robert Van Amsted's. Emmy's father, who'd treated him like his own son since they'd first met so many years ago. He'd made it clear he always wished Emmy had had enough sense to marry Aidan instead of "that wishy-washy fool" she had married.

"I hear there's been a mix-up with the accommodations there, but don't worry about it. Just want you to know you're still welcome to stay there as long as you want. Don't let that girl of mine bully you out of the place."

That girl... Aidan was no stranger to the rift between Emmy and her father. They were two headstrong people who never should have been cursed with being in the same family. Emmy had never forgiven her father for being a womanizer during his marriage to her mother, and Robert had never forgiven Emmy for being so far out of his control.

The machine clicked off, and Aidan reached over and pressed Delete. While his hand was still near the curtain, on a whim he pushed it to the side just enough to see out, and he caught sight of Emmy bending over to examine something her son was studying on the ground, her beautiful ass right there for Aidan to admire.

Damn it. There his fool body went again.

WHEN HE was sure his mother was sleeping, Max crept out of his sleeping bag on the couch and went to the window. He wasn't afraid of the dark like some other kids.

He liked to pretend he was a cat creeping around in

the darkness, hunting for prey. Well, except he didn't like to hunt. He just liked to explore. He wished he could go outside and explore in the dark like a cat, but he knew his mom would be way too mad if he did that.

So he watched from the window, hoping he would get to see some nighttime animal out there, maybe a possum or an owl, or even a coyote if he got real lucky. He knew all about nocturnal animals from a book he'd gotten at the library called *Creatures of the Night.*

But all he could see outside were trees and stars and the almost-full moon. He looked across the yard at the cabin where the pirate was staying.

His mom hadn't given him any good reason for there being a pirate in his grandma's cabin. She'd laughed when he asked about the intruder and said that he wasn't a pirate at all, just a regular man.

But Max didn't think his mom would know a pirate when she saw one, and she didn't really understand that when he called the man a pirate, it didn't actually matter if he had a peg leg or a ship of his own. It was more interesting to imagine things than to go around believing stuff that really happened.

She'd said the man was writing a book, which made Max even more curious. He liked books, and he had never thought to wonder where they came from before, or that actual pirates might sit down and write all the words to make a book.

He decided right then and there that he wanted to write a book, too. He'd write about being a pirate and finding a treasure here at Promise Lake. Maybe he would make it a guide for people who wanted to hunt for treasure. People didn't know about freshwater pirates and their treasures, so it would be good to write a story about them.

Max liked telling stories. He made them up in his head all the time when he wasn't reading or exploring, because then he could think about happy things instead of sad stuff like about his dad being gone all the way to Tibet.

He wondered if the pirate in his grandma's cabin was sleeping now, or if he was sitting in the dark writing about being a pirate. Max remembered the scar he had on his face, and he decided the pirate must have been writing a story about how he'd gotten that scar.

Maybe he'd fought off an alligator, or gotten in a sword fight with a sailor, or been forced to walk the plank. Maybe he'd had to come here and hide out because of the treasure he'd stolen from some other bad guy.

Through the tall redwoods, he could see the big dark place where the lake was. The moonlight made the little waves on the lake look silver, and Max imagined a pirate ship sailing up to their shore, and the pirate climbing out and burying his treasure right there in the front yard.

Max would start looking for it tomorrow, but he'd have to be careful not to let the pirate see him search.

CHAPTER THREE

When I woke up, I found myself lying on the floor of a small filthy room. I was alone, and my hands and feet were bound with rope. My entire body throbbed with pain, but especially my head. I felt as if an army of men had taken turns beating the life out of me, which, I later learned, was exactly what had happened.

From *Through a Soldier's Eyes*
by Aidan Caldwell

EMMY PEERED across the dusty shelves of People Food, the local food co-op, and smiled at the familiar face she spotted in the next aisle.

"Ben?" she said to her playmate from summers long past, as happy memories flooded her head. This was part of the reason she'd come back to Promise, because it was full of people who'd been connected to some of the most carefree times of her life. And because it was one of those rare small towns filled with open-minded oddballs who believed in letting people live their lives however they chose without judgment.

A head full of blond dreadlocks ducked to a gap in

between boxes of organic pasta. "Emmy! My girl, where the hell have you been?"

He straightened and came around to her aisle, then embraced her in a bear hug. She laughed and hugged him back. At her side, Max had his nose buried in a small field guide to animals of northern California and showed no notice of anything around him.

"Whoa, is this your boy?" Ben said when he spotted her half-sized companion.

"Yes, this is my son, Max. He's six."

Ben squatted and regarded the child seriously. "I'm sorry to interrupt your reading, little man. I'm Ben."

Max looked up at him absently. "Hi," he muttered, then went right back to reading.

"You here for the summer?"

"We're here for good," Emmy said, and Ben beamed.

"Excellent. Hey, little man—one last interruption. Maybe I can take you out for a hike to check out some of those animals in person sometime. Sound good?"

Max finally gave Ben his full attention. "Yeah. I saw a red-tailed hawk already, and a turkey vulture and an Axis deer. But I really want to see some snakes. Do you know how to find snakes?"

"Absolutely. I'll hook you up."

Ben stood and smiled at Emmy. "Wow. So you're a mom now. Intense."

She smiled and sensed it made her look a little weary. She'd never intended to be a *single* mom. So far, the reality of it was not as bad as she'd feared at her most insecure moments before the divorce, but it still didn't fit with the perfect-happy-family image she'd pictured back when she'd been pregnant with Max. She was beginning to understand that when her dreams crumbled, she had to pick up the pieces and build something new with them.

"Yep," she said. "How about you?"

"No kids for me yet, but someday. I'm still trying to convince Anouk that I'm the guy for her," he said, smiling wryly. He'd been after gorgeous Anouk Samms for as long as Emmy could remember. The universe would never be the same if he ever stopped chasing her or she ever stood still long enough to be caught.

At the front of the store, a woman hovered near the register waiting for help.

"Just a sec," Ben said to Emmy. "Don't go anywhere—I want to catch up," he said as he went to the register.

He knew the woman who was checking out as well, apparently, and the two chatted as Emmy continued to fill her shopping basket with enough food to last a few days. She had missed this place more than she realized. She'd missed the camaraderie of knowing all her neighbors and bumping into friends everywhere she went in town. It could get claustrophobic at times, but the benefits far outweighed the occasional annoyances.

Promise was one of those rare small vacation towns where progressive values and civic-mindedness kept the community vibrant and close-knit both during tourist season and in the quieter winter months. It didn't exist for the tourists, but rather, it made their vacations far more interesting than a town full of generic restaurants and tchotchke shops would have.

Emmy selected some organic cherries, a couple of navel oranges and the makings for a big salad, then stood agonizing over boxes of snack food for Max, trying to decide which ones didn't fall too far into the category of junk food.

"So what brings you back to the promised land?" Ben asked, using their old sarcastic name for the place, as he approached her again. "I thought you were a famous architect now or something. If I had a TV, I'd have checked you out on that house network or whatever it is."

He was referring to a short stint Emmy had done hosting a show on famous houses, right after she'd quit her job at the architectural firm but before she'd decided to chuck that whole life altogether.

"I gave up my job in San Francisco," she explained. "Also recently went through a divorce."

"Oh yeah! I think I heard about that in the newspaper or something, right?"

Emmy nodded.

"Pretty crazy when your personal life ends up in the news."

She winced. "*Crazy* is one word for it."

Steven's family was one of San Francisco's wealthiest, and he was one of the city's golden boys. Their divorce had, unfortunately, made the news, much to Emmy's horror.

He nodded solemnly. "I hear you. So what have you been up to?"

"I started homeschooling Max, because he was having some trouble with starting kindergarten on the heels of his dad and me splitting up." And his dad was running off on a spiritual quest, she left out.

"Cool. And you're here to stay? Moving into your family's—" He stopped short.

"That was my intention, at least for a while, but I didn't realize my dad had loaned the place out until I got here. We're staying in the guest cottage for now."

"You know that dude who's staying there?"

"Aidan? Yeah, we used to date, oddly enough."

Understanding dawned on Ben's face. "Wait—did he come here with you one summer?"

"Yep."

"I thought he looked kinda familiar. Anyway, he seems a little odd, never leaves that place. Has all his food delivered."

"You might have also seen *him* in the news. He was one of the peacekeepers involved in that famous kidnapping and escape in Darfur."

"Wow. That's intense."

"I imagine it had an effect on him."

Emmy thought of the haunted look in Aidan's eyes. She hadn't seen whatever had wiped away the idealism in his eyes and replaced it with something darker. She didn't know what kind of ghosts he lived with now that their lives had taken such different paths, though somehow those paths had brought them around to the same place.

Ben rubbed his beard and nodded solemnly. "So

what about you then? You can't stay in that little guest cottage forever."

"I'm getting back in touch with my passion for green architecture. I'm going to build a place for me and Max on my parents' property."

"Whoa! That's excellent."

She nodded. "I'm excited."

"You need a carpenter, I'm your man."

"I might take you up on that. I was thinking of you, actually. I'm going to start working independently as a green architect, and it would help to have connections in the building industry."

"Like, designing eco-friendly houses?"

Emmy nodded. "I think there'll be enough of a market here for people who need to renovate their existing houses along with anyone who wants to build a new place. I'm hoping to make a niche for myself in small houses between maybe a hundred and a thousand square feet."

"I'm digging that. I saw this little place down in Sonoma County—a ninety-six square-foot house for two."

Emmy smiled. She knew and loved that designer's work—tiny houses that made maximum use of space and understood the beauty of efficiency. "That's the kind of thing I'm talking about, but on a family-sized scale."

She took a business card out of her wallet and handed it to Ben. "Do you have a phone?"

"Yep, I finally joined the twenty-first century and got

a cell phone a few months ago, actually." He went to the counter and wrote his number on a piece of paper, then came back and handed it to her.

"I'll get in touch with you soon as I'm settled in, then." And for the first time since she'd arrived, she felt the slightest little bit of hope that things weren't going to be ridiculously difficult at every turn.

She grabbed a box of organic ginger cookies, then followed Ben to the register, where a poster for the annual Promise Fest hung on the front of the counter. The date for it was two weekends away. "You going to be at the festival?" she asked.

"Absolutely. I'm playing guitar in Tom Jackson's reggae band on the first day of it. You should check us out."

Emmy smiled. "I will."

A festival to mark the start of their new lives was perfect. She'd always loved the funky event that began with a parade of the local eccentrics and civic organizations down Main Street, and went on all weekend with food, music and general merriment. It would be a chance for her to reconnect with the community.

Her new-found lightheartedness at bumping into Ben lasted all of five minutes as she drove toward the cabin. She spotted the unwelcome motorcycle in the driveway, Aidan popped into her head, and her illusory good mood vanished into thin air.

AIDAN'S HANDS were shaking again. Emmy seemed to have that effect on him now. He simultaneously wanted to strip her down and make love to her, and run away to hide from her and the maddening power she had over him.

God, he'd turned into such a freak.

He peered out the crack in the curtains at Emmy, across the redwood grove in the clearing near the lake, talking to a man he didn't recognize. The man held a notepad on a clipboard and made occasional notes on it. They were staking out a rectangular space...a building site.

She'd been here only a day and a half, and she was already planning to build something?

Aidan's stomach pitched. A building site would mean people, and hammering and machinery. His quiet little prison would be transformed into a new, intolerable one. He'd come here to escape the noise of people and civilization, not to be immersed in it.

And leaving here was not an option, regardless of what Emmy thought. It had been a month since he'd even stepped beyond the front porch.

His heart thudded in his ears as he watched the man walk back to his truck, climb into it and drive away. Emmy still stood in the clearing with her arms crossed, looking at the staked-out space. It was probably two hundred steps from where he sat now to where she stood, and part of him wanted to run from here to there, screaming, "No! Stop! You can't build a house there!"

But he sat frozen.

A movement from the corner of his eye caught his attention. It was the kid, scrounging around in the dirt, a pine cone in one hand and a stick in the other. He was peering at something on the side of a tree now, hunched down watching as if it was the most interesting thing he'd ever seen.

Aidan felt something tugging inside of him as he watched the boy. Some dormant longing that he hadn't felt in years and didn't want to contemplate now.

Max had Emmy's dark hair and green eyes, and her porcelain skin, too. He was a carbon copy of her in boy form, with a coating of dust and a perpetual cowlick on the back of his head.

Aidan clenched his eyes shut at a sudden burning sensation in his gut. He muttered a curse and stood, paced across the room and back again. He felt like a caged animal, like the way he imagined a tiger raised in a zoo would feel, both longing for freedom and terrified when presented with the reality of it.

All he had to do was unlock the door, open it, walk across the yard and through the redwoods to where Emmy stood. Tell her why she could not upset this little place of quiet that was his last hope for sanity. But he knew, too, that unless she had changed in the years since they'd been together, she wouldn't simply back down.

It would never be that easy.

He peered through the curtain at her again. And then, as if she'd been reading his thoughts, she turned and headed straight for the cabin. She couldn't see him, but she was looking right at the window where he stood.

A few moments later, there was a determined knock at his door.

"Aidan?" she called. "I need to talk to you."

He took a few deep breaths and forced himself to cross the room again. This was his chance to set her straight. Right here, right now, no backing down. He jerked open the door, and before he could block her way, she stepped inside and looked around.

But he could only watch her, lithe and beautiful in her movements, her presence filling up the house with everything it lacked. His body responded in a primal way to her, and it took all his concentration not to imagine taking her in his arms and kissing her, inappropriate as it would have been. He marveled that she could have such a strong effect on him, even at a time like this.

"This place hasn't changed," she said. "Not in twenty years."

"What were you doing out there?" he said by way of greeting.

She crossed her arms over her chest and set her mouth in an expression he knew meant she was preparing for an argument. "That's what I came to talk to you about. I'm prepping that site to build on, and excavation will begin tomorrow."

"Excavation?" he repeated dully.

She nodded. "I applied for the permits months ago, and I found someone to build the foundation, but some prep work needs to happen first. That'll start tomorrow."

"Prep work." He could feel himself breaking into a cold sweat.

"I'd planned to go at a more leisurely pace, but since

you don't want to move out of this place and Max and I can't live in the guest cottage for long, I figure I might as well get things rolling since I found a contractor available to help me out."

"You can't have people coming around here so soon."

Emmy was looking at him oddly now. "Is something wrong? You look like you're about to pass out."

He wiped at his forehead, feeling as though he needed to sit down. "You should go," he said. "I—I…"

Can't talk now, he'd intended to say, but instead, black-and-white fuzz, like a TV screen with no reception, covered his vision, a sudden wave of nausea crashed into his gut, and he had the sensation of falling.

The next thing he knew was opening his eyes to Emmy peering down at him, looking worried.

"Aidan? Can you hear me?" she said. "Should I call 911 or something?"

He blinked up at the ceiling. "No, I'm okay. I'm just…a little…" A little what? A little crazy? A little unable to deal with normal things like going outside and talking to other humans anymore?

What?

"I'm going to get you some water," she said, taking a pillow from the couch and wedging it under his head without asking.

He closed his eyes again and tried to will his head to stop spinning. So, he'd just passed out? That hadn't happened before. Well, not since the little cement-floored room that he tried to forget. Not since the days of men's voices crying out, and pain so intense his mind had chosen to shut off rather than stay conscious for it.

Those had been his first experiences with passing out. And now he was hitting the floor like a two-hundred-pound Scarlett O'Hara without the corset? Over the thought of some noise and people?

Damn it. His weakness was repulsive even to him— he could only imagine how disgusting it looked to Emmy.

She reappeared and knelt beside him. He didn't open his eyes, but he could feel her there next him, waiting.

"Have you seen a doctor about this…this condition?" she said.

"I don't have a condition." He opened his eyes and sat up. He felt better now. Somehow the passing out had been like hitting the reset button on his body's ability to handle stress.

"Oh, really?" She was staring at him curiously. "You're sweating. It's sixty-eight degrees in here. I just checked on the wall thermometer."

He took the water but didn't drink it. "I'm fine."

"I could drive you into town to the doctor there, if you don't feel well enough to drive."

"No!" he said too sharply.

She didn't look intimidated though. Emmy never did.

"Aidan, what's really going on? Does this have to do with what you experienced in Darfur?"

The black-and-white fuzz was filling his vision

again. He squeezed his eyes shut and leaned back against the side of the couch. "Maybe," he finally said. "I don't know."

"Post traumatic stress disorder?"

"Yeah, but…" But it was worse than that now. He'd gotten worse, not better.

"But what?"

"I don't know. Forget it."

She frowned, and he found himself staring at her mouth as if it was the key to his salvation.

Her lips were full, an impossibly soft pink color, and her mouth was wide in a way that made her smile look endless when it appeared. It just went on forever. And he used to kiss her as often as he could. He'd kiss her hello and goodbye and for no reason at all. He'd kiss her until she laughed and pushed him away because she was trying to study or read a book, but more often than not, they'd end up laughing and making love.

Making love. How long had it been? He had not been with a woman in a year and a half, at least. He'd stopped living, stopped doing all the things that had once made life good.

"I think you should let me take you to the doct—"

He leaned forward and kissed her.

He hadn't meant to do it. Hadn't thought of the wisdom of it. He'd just gone for her mouth as if there might be some salvation there. Caught off guard, she hadn't kissed him back at first. She simply sat there, shocked.

But then he felt her opening up to him, her lips parting for his tongue to find hers. His whole body caught fire then, and he pulled her against him, into his lap. His hands were holding onto her as if she were his life preserver.

She smelled exactly as she always had, like honeysuckle and woman, and he wanted her naked body against his. Wanted to bury himself inside her and never come back out.

She'd be his refuge from this world.

Where once they'd been too young and passionate and intense, now they could get it right. They'd have heartbreak and maturity to lead them down a better path together.

But a moment later, the spell was broken.

"Mom?" a child's voice called from outside.

Emmy stiffened and pulled herself away. She looked stunned by the kiss, and her gaze searched his for some answer about what had just happened.

"I'll be right back," she said and scrambled to her feet, then rushed out the front door.

He could hear her talking to her son, telling him she'd be free to go swimming in a little while, that he could put on his trunks but had to stay here near the house until she was ready to go.

Aidan stared down at the glass of water that lay sideways on the floor next to him, its contents forming a dark spot on the red Pakistani rug. He didn't remember dropping it, but he must have. The energy to get up and take care of the spill eluded him.

Emmy came into the room and sighed. "What was that?" she asked as she knelt beside him again.

"A kiss for old times' sake?" He'd meant it as a joke but didn't have the energy to even smile now.

"I don't want Max to see anything like that and get the wrong idea. He's still getting used to his dad being gone from his life. I don't want to make things harder on him."

"Sure. Of course," Aidan said dully.

"And, of course, I—I mean, we…didn't work out the first time around. There aren't any lingering feelings… you know?"

He might have relieved the awkwardness by saying something, but he stared silently. He didn't know. He had lingering feelings, maybe not many good ones, but certainly he had feelings where she was concerned. He'd loved her in a way he'd never had the courage or the foolhardiness to love anyone since.

She'd been the one to teach him to guard his heart, the one who'd made him understand what the word *heartbroken* meant, the one who'd forced him to change the channel on the radio when sad love songs came on.

Unfortunately, he feared, she still had the power to undo him.

Her brow was creased with worry. "What's going on with you, Aidan?"

"I think it's called agoraphobia," he blurted. "I don't really go outside or anything anymore."

"Wow." She sat silent, pondering what he'd said.

"You can't have people coming around here, or noise. I—I know it sounds crazy, but I can't handle it."

His heart started pounding faster, thudding in his ears until it drowned out all other sound.

She shook her head. "I'm sorry, Aidan. I came here to build a house. My new business depends on it. And that's what I'm going to do."

CHAPTER FOUR

We didn't know when it was day or night. Hours ticked by in slow motion, and days faded into one another without beginning or end. Coming unhinged from time became a torture of its own. I fought against it by counting the shift changes of our captors, and the meals we were fed, and I could roughly estimate the passage of time in this way.

From *Through a Soldier's Eyes*
by Aidan Caldwell

"MAMA, what's wrong with that man in grandma's house?"

"What do you mean, honey?" Emmy asked, though her thoughts immediately went back to the kiss she and Aidan had shared last week.

She'd been haunted by that kiss, tormented, brought awake at night tense and longing for things she didn't have. It had been a taste of the intensity she didn't dare go near again in this lifetime. Her immature self had loved Aidan, but her mature self, the one that had been forced to grow up and learn to put her child first, could not go back to being the girl she had been, or loving the way she used to.

She stood at the small sink in the guest cottage washing dishes. The sink was overflowing from the day's breakfast and lunch dishes, as if trying to point out to her that this place was too small for the two of them to share.

They could only store a few days' groceries in the efficiency refrigerator and cabinets, and Emmy, just two days into the house-building project and a little more than a week into staying in the cottage, was painfully aware of her lack of a dedicated work space. She longed for a desk where she could spread out her designs without fear of dirty fingers grabbing things or a half-drunk cup of milk overturning on her computer.

Just that morning, Max had put a wet, muddy rock on a copy of her blueprints, and she'd yelled at him, then immediately regretted it and apologized. Even Aidan's presence in the next house, although they hadn't seen him in a day and a half, felt as if it was causing the walls to close in on her.

"Why is he so mad?"

She set a plate on the drainer that took up half their useable counter space and turned to look at him. "Did he say something to you?"

Max gazed at her warily, a dirty old femur bone of some unidentified forest animal in his hand. "No," he said, clearly uncertain why she was taking such an interest in his question.

"Why do you think he's mad then?"

"Because he looks mad and he doesn't come outside," he said simply, and Emmy felt like an idiot for thinking it was more complicated than that.

It was true they hadn't seen Aidan do anything but scowl since they'd arrived—that is, when they had actually seen him, which wasn't often. And Max had a great sense of intuition, but he could also wonder about simpler things like why a grown-up might look so angry all the time when he peered out the window at them.

"Do you think he forgot where he buried his treasure?"

"His what?"

"His treasure," Max said matter-of-factly.

Emmy had gotten used to her son's seemingly non-sensical comments, and she knew how to backtrack and figure out where his leaps of logic came from. Usually.

"You mean like pirate treasure?"

"Yeah."

"You still think Aidan is a pirate?"

"Isn't he?"

She bit her lip, tried not to smile. "I can see why you might think that, but it's more likely he's just a regular guy."

Max looked at her as if he pitied her for her lack of imagination, and he was probably right to do so.

Max sighed. "I'm bored, Mom."

"Bored? Why don't you go outside and play?"

"I want some other kids to play with."

That was the biggest problem with living here in the

woods. The nearest neighbor kid wasn't in go-next-door-and-knock distance.

"We can go to the beach later. There might be some kids there."

"But I want someone to play with now."

"I'm sorry, sweetie, but I have things around here to get done first."

Another heavy sigh. "Why'd we have to move here, anyway?"

"I thought you liked it here."

He said nothing, but stared morosely at the femur bone.

Emmy had worried about whether homeschooling Max would isolate him too much, and now that she was trying to get their house built *and* launch her business, she was getting the sense that she'd taken on too much, and something would have to give.

"How would you feel about going to a summer day camp?" she asked.

"What's that?"

"It would be a place you could go to play with other kids, do fun stuff, make things, go on outdoor adventures—"

"Yeah, I want to go there. Can we go now?"

"No, I have to sign you up. The other good thing is, it could give you a chance to meet kids you might want to go to school with in the fall."

"School? You mean like not being homeschooled anymore?"

Emmy nodded. "How do you feel about that?"

He gave the matter some thought. "Yeah, I want to go to regular school again, as long as it's not boring."

"I think I can find you an interesting school where you'll have fun, okay?"

"All right, but I'm still bored right now."

"I don't want to hear you talking like that. There's no such thing as bored."

"Does that mean there's no such thing as fun, either?"

She tried not to laugh. Max never failed to poke holes in her shaky arguments.

"All I mean is, it's up to you to entertain yourself. If you're bored, you do something about it. Why don't you go outside and collect pine cones or something?"

Max sighed yet again, playing the drama queen, but he got up and went outside, slamming the door behind himself. Emmy thought of following after him to warn him about slamming doors, but she decided to pick her battles. At least she had a few moments alone now.

She'd been feeling keyed up and anxious ever since arriving at the lake. So much was at stake right now, and she wasn't as sure as she'd been a few weeks ago that she could really handle it all—especially not when factoring in the ever-nagging presence of Aidan.

Even though he was usually out of sight, he was rarely out of Emmy's mind. He was a constant reminder of the stupid girl she'd once been, a person she couldn't respect and couldn't imagine being again. She'd been selfish, self-centered, a spoiled brat. She liked who she was now—a mother, an architect, a woman matured by life experience—and she hated the feelings Aidan evoked that reminded her of the person she used to be.

Aside from the stress of having her past living next door to her, the contractor was already proving to be a bit of a prima donna in his resistance to her ideas. The construction crew she'd counted on putting through training so they could understand her unconventional building methods were being resistant, too, and aside from her friend Ben, whom she'd asked the contractor to hire as a carpenter, they were uninterested in learning anything new.

As if that wasn't enough stress, the cost of building materials kept going up as her budget kept shrinking, and she was afraid she was going to run out of money if she didn't get hired soon to build a house for someone else.

Not to mention single motherhood and her lack of a social life.

And Aidan's kiss was a painful reminder of the lack of physical pleasure in her life right now. She'd felt it in places she hadn't wanted to feel it, and dormant parts of herself had woken up and begun to tingle.

Divorce had killed her sense of romance about life. Other than one brief, frantic, insane relationship she'd had while going through the thick of her divorce misery, she'd avoided men. She hadn't wanted the pain or the complication, not when she was struggling to stay sane and balanced for Max's sake. And not when she wasn't even sure she'd cleaned up all the pieces of her shattered heart.

So it was a revelation to be feeling something like desire again, something like attraction. She felt as if she were waking up to that part of life, but if so, she was waking up to the wrong person.

She wondered how much of her apparent attraction to Aidan had to do with feeling sorry for him for what he'd been through. He must have suffered horribly as a hostage, and judging by the look in his eyes and his erratic behavior, he suffered still. She wanted to help, but how?

She thought of her old friend Lydia Cormier, whom she'd known since childhood and who still lived in Promise. She'd heard Lydia had worked with soldiers returning from war in her psychology practice. Maybe…if Aidan would talk to a therapist, he might find some healing.

As she finished washing the last few dishes, she made a mental note to get Lydia's contact information.

She had to help Aidan somehow, and that was at least a start. And, she believed he could use a friend. Perhaps she wasn't the best choice of friend for him, given their history, but she would find ways to look out for him if she could. That's what a friend would do.

No matter how much she wanted to help though, she couldn't let herself be attracted to Aidan. He was mentally unbalanced, and he was an unwelcome ghost from her past. She'd come to Promise Lake to get a fresh start, to take care of herself and her son, not to relive past mistakes. She and Aidan had been too intense together, and she didn't want that kind of energy in her life again.

She'd just have to keep reminding herself of that until she believed it with her mind *and* her heart.

AIDAN HAD MANAGED over a week of having Emmy and her kid living right next door, while mostly avoiding them. He'd developed coping mechanisms, like wearing his iPod headphones with the music on when they were making noise, and keeping the curtains closed if he got sick of seeing them moving about. But their presence stayed wedged in his consciousness like a thorn in his side, so that he could never quite forget about them and feel at peace.

And, speaking of interruptions, someone was knocking at the door. He looked up from his computer and muttered a curse. Just when he was finally getting rolling a bit—he'd written a whole sentence—of course there was an interruption.

But he'd ordered groceries that morning, and he couldn't very well ignore the grocery delivery person. He needed food.

He went to the door and made the mistake of not looking through the window before opening it, because there on the porch stood the kid, Max, staring up at him.

The boy didn't bother with hello, but said, simply, "Did you know a ghost lives here?"

"What?"

"My cousin Dylan told me a ghost lives here."

Aidan's first reaction was to roll his eyes. Robert Van Amsted had told him the same thing when he'd offered Aidan the cabin. Some nonsense about his aunt who'd died in the lake and whose spirit stuck around rearranging dishes and rustling through the curtains. He'd insisted she was harmless, and Aidan had figured, what the hell, a ghost was probably the only company he could tolerate at this point in his life.

Before, he might not have believed in ghosts, but he'd seen enough unjust death in his life not to dismiss such ideas completely anymore.

Still, he'd never seen even the slightest hint of otherworldly spirits at the cabin. The ghost story had turned out to be just that.

"Sorry to disappoint you, but there's no ghost here."

"How do you know?"

"Look, kid, you need to get lost. I'm working right now."

"Then why did you answer the door?"

Aidan cursed under his breath, then said, "Because I thought you were the grocery delivery person."

"Why don't you go out to buy your groceries?"

"Why do you ask so many questions?"

The boy frowned and took a step back, finally getting the message that he wasn't wanted here. "Maybe the ghost is scared of you and that's why you never see her."

"Then she's a smart ghost."

"How come you look mad all the time?"

"Kid, get lost."

But the child didn't budge any farther. Aidan grasped his arm gently but firmly, then nudged him backward until he could close and lock the door.

Alone again, he shook his head and went back to the desk. Damn rug rat. He'd have to let Emmy know now that he wasn't going to tolerate any more kid interruptions. Next time, he wasn't going to be so gentle about telling the kid to get the hell out of here.

But the thought of having to talk to her again made his face turn hot and his throat close up. He stood and went to the bathroom, flicked on the light, and bent over the sink as he turned the water on. He splashed cold water on his face, then cupped his hand under the faucet and drank a few gulps. He was breathing hard, and he needed to calm down before he went into a full-on panic attack.

Okay, he had to think calm, soothing thoughts. Water... ocean...beach...crashing waves... He pictured a rugged, quiet beach at Point Reyes, a place that had always drawn him and soothed him. Imagined himself there, cold water lapping at his feet, sunlight dancing off wet sand, making it look as if the beach were covered in diamonds. He would have given anything to be a normal person who could go there right now instead of cowering here inside a cabin, afraid of the ghosts in his head he couldn't escape.

His thoughts were interrupted by the noise of the bulldozer outside. Freaking wonderful. That meant lunch break was done and he had another four hours of construction noise to endure before there would be any peace and quiet again.

Then there was another knock at the door, this one louder and more insistent than the first. Okay, definitely the grocery delivery guy. Even so, he considered ignoring it. But he needed food, he reminded himself.

He had exactly one can of chicken noodle soup left in the cupboard.

Aidan dried his face, took a few deep breaths, and headed back into the living room.

This time, he remembered to look through the front window, peeking through a crack in the curtain, to see who was on the front porch. Not the grocery guy, but Emmy, looking furious.

He wasn't going to answer. His throat was already constricting again, and he instinctively headed toward the bedroom, wanting to put as much distance between her and him as possible.

"Answer the door, Aidan! I know you can hear me!"

Big problem with being afraid to leave the house—everyone knew where he was all the goddamn time.

He grabbed his iPod from the desk and was about to put the ear buds in and blast the music as loudly as he could stand it when he heard Emmy say, "I've got a key to this place, you know. I'll come in if you don't open up."

His panic turned to fury, and he rounded on the door, stormed back to it and jerked it open.

"Don't ever invade my privacy," he said in a voice so deadly serious, Emmy managed to look a bit apprehensive—for a split second, anyway.

"Don't *you* ever lay a hand on my son again!" As she spoke, she jabbed a finger at his chest, and on the third jab, she made contact.

He looked down at the offending finger, attached to her long, elegant hand, and he felt the fury drain from him. She was just a mother protecting her child. Any good parent would have done the same. The kid had probably lied to her about the extent of Aidan having nudged him out the door.

Her hand dropped to her side then, and he looked back at her face.

"I didn't hurt your kid," he said.

"You can't grab him and force him to do what you want."

"All I did was gently guide him out the door."

Her expression showed warring emotions—fury being replaced by doubt. "If that's true, next time, don't touch him at all. Then there won't be any debate."

"*Next time?* How about next time, the kid stays the hell away from my door and leaves me alone?"

"I understand you don't want to be bothered. I'll make sure he knows he's not to knock on this door again unless there's an emergency."

"Not even if there's an emergency. No knocking—period."

"That's ridiculous. What if your house is burning down?"

"Then I'd better get the hell out. But I don't need a six-year-old to tell me so."

"You're the nearest available adult besides me. If he's hurt and needs help, I'd like to know that you would at least assist him."

Aidan bit his cheek to keep from saying anything stupid. Of course the kid should be able to come to him for help. He wasn't a heartless monster. But still some sick part of him rebelled against the idea.

He forced himself to say, "Sure, yeah, if it's an emergency and he needs help. Otherwise, no more interruptions."

"Listen," Emmy said, sounding calmer now. "I've been thinking about what you told me, about how you're suffering from agoraphobia…and I've been meaning to talk to you, because I know a therapist in town who might be able to help."

She held a business card out to him, and he felt like a fool. Was he really the kind of person people needed to gently refer to therapists?

Of course he was.

He took the card and stared at the name on it. Lydia Cormier, Doctor of Psychology.

"She's an old friend of mine. She's worked with soldiers and others who've come back from war zones, so I thought…"

Her voice trailed off, and Aidan looked up at her.

Emmy was looking at him as if she both pitied him and loathed him. She was about to say something else when they were interrupted yet again by a kid's voice calling, "Mommy, Mommy!"

The scrawny boy came running across the driveway from the direction of the construction site. He stopped when he had their attention.

"A treasure chest!" he called out, looking as if they were the most exciting two words he'd ever uttered. "The bulldozer found a treasure chest!"

CHAPTER FIVE

I used to laugh at the phrase *peacekeeping force*.
Is it possible to force peace in any meaningful
way? I still don't know the true answer to that
question.

From *Through a Soldier's Eyes*
by Aidan Caldwell

EMMY LOOKED at the dark wood chest, probably a foot and
a half wide by a foot deep and tall, still caked with dirt
after being unearthed by the bulldozer while digging out
the foundation for the house, and she felt a weird fluttering in her belly. It wasn't just Max's odd insistence that
this lake was inhabited by pirates, or that the chest did
resemble a pirate chest with its brass fixtures and heavy
brass lock, or that Max had claimed Aidan himself was a
pirate, or even that Max had been bent on hunting for a
treasure for the past week. It was... She didn't know
what.

Odd.

Very odd.

It touched upon the faintest memory she had from
childhood, some story she'd been told perhaps, but she
couldn't quite put her finger on what it was.

This property had belonged to her family since soon after the Gold Rush, when one of her ancestors had taken his earnings and bought up land he'd deemed investment-worthy all over northern California. He'd had exquisite taste, and the Van Amsted family was lucky to still own some of the best lots, like this jewel of redwood-dotted paradise on the shore of Promise Lake.

So the chest most likely had belonged to someone in her family. But why would it have been buried? And why here, so far away from the main house?

The fluttering in her belly turned into a full-on sense of dread as she turned over possibilities. Images of infant corpses or shameful family secrets crowded her head. Whatever this was, it was probably something someone had wanted to keep hidden.

"Mom, look, it's locked like a real pirate chest. Do you think we can figure out how to open it?"

Before she could answer, a white van with a People Food logo—a rainbow over the lake, with a psychedelic font for the name—pulled into the driveway. She watched as a woman she didn't recognize got out and carried two bags of groceries to Aidan's front porch.

This time, he opened the door without any drama, but his gaze brushed over them and the treasure chest before he turned his attention to the delivery woman.

Emmy's anger at him had quickly dissipated when she'd realized he wasn't thinking like a normal person. He was mentally ill, and he needed help. Max had been told always to let her know if any adult touched him at all—ever—and when he'd said Aidan had grabbed him by the arm and made him leave the cabin, she'd been furious.

But she didn't believe Aidan had meant any harm, and Max didn't have so much as a fingerprint from the incident.

As much as she found Aidan's presence unpleasant and irritating, she still wanted to help him.

But that would have to wait. For now, she had a mystery chest and a little boy dying to know if it held any ancient treasures.

"I'm not sure how we'll open the chest, honey," Emmy said, distracted. "There's probably a way to cut the lock."

Nearby, the contractor, Frank, was listening. He came over and bent to take a closer look at the hardware on the chest. "Looks like you could just take it apart at the hinges with a screwdriver," he offered.

"Do you have one handy?"

"Sure do. Let me get it off my truck." And with that, he headed for the driveway.

The woman was climbing back into the driver's seat of the van by then, and when Emmy looked over at the cabin, she saw Aidan hovering in the doorway, still watching them. Given the rest of his recent behavior, she would have expected him to slam the door shut as soon as he could, but he hadn't.

He was staring at the chest now, apparently fascinated. As was everyone on the construction site.

When Frank returned, he handed Emmy the screwdriver and said to his crew, "All right everyone. Show's over. Back to work."

To Emmy he said, "Let me help you move this away from the site. Where would you like it?"

She tested its weight. "It's okay. I can carry it, but thanks."

She tucked the screwdriver into her back pocket and picked up the chest by its two metal handles, which were still caked with dirt and corroded from probably decades in the cold, damp earth.

"I knew it. I knew there was a pirate chest! I knew it!" Max chanted over and over as he followed her across the property.

Emmy should have taken the chest right past the cabin to the guest cottage, but Aidan still lingered in his doorway, and when she thought of how he hadn't come outside since she'd arrived she felt horrible for him. Here he was in one of the most beautiful places in the world, and he couldn't even enjoy it. He didn't seem to be enjoying anything about his life.

She made up her mind in that moment about what she would do, stopping in front of the cabin. "I could use a little help opening this," she lied. "If you don't mind."

He stared at the chest, seemingly torn between his curiosity about it and his fear of going outside.

"I..." he said, looking pale.

Had she pushed him too far with that simple request? Was he going to have another panic attack?

"Could I bring it up onto the porch?"

His gaze darted over at the workers on the construction site, and she realized he didn't want a crowd around to witness his emergence into the world.

"How about the back steps...where it's sunnier and warm?"

That would be out of sight of the men working on the foundation, and it would be a little quieter, too.

It seemed as if he couldn't say anything, so she decided to make the decision for him. "I'll bring this around back," she said and headed toward the side of the house before he could protest.

"But, Mommy...what if it's his treasure chest? Won't he be mad that we found it?"

"Perhaps," she said vaguely.

Emmy hadn't considered the possibility that the chest she was holding might belong to Aidan. That would explain his intense interest in it.... And his fury over where she'd chosen to build the house.

But no, surely if it had belonged to him, he'd have had the sense to dig it up before construction began. Unless he'd been too afraid to leave the house, thanks to his illness. Or he'd forgotten where he'd buried it....

Well, they'd find out soon enough.

She rounded the corner of the house and went to the rear steps, then set the chest down. Aidan had probably figured out by now that she knew how to operate a screwdriver and didn't really need his help, but she fully intended to stand here looking helpless until he opened the door and came out.

This late-June day was one of the most beautiful she'd witnessed in ages, and she didn't want him to miss it. The air was a perfect seventy-five degrees, and the slightest breeze came off the lake, just enough to keep the sun from feeling too hot. The sky was a perfect crystalline blue, and light danced off the azure lake like diamonds floating on the surface.

This was the kind of day that made her feel as if she were a little girl again, running through the forest pretending to be a fairy, her hands and knees dirty, her hair hanging to her waist. She'd play with her siblings and cousins and friends all day, diving into the lake whenever they got hot, then play some more.

Why did adulthood so rarely contain such pure, unencumbered joy?

Max was dancing around now in that excited little way he had, bouncing and fidgeting. "C'mon, Mommy, what are you waiting for? Let's open it!"

"I'd like Aidan to tell us if it's his or not before we try to open it. Like you said, he might get mad…"

She tapped gently on the back door, and inside, she heard footsteps, but nothing else. Somewhere nearby, a woodpecker worked away at a tree. Max heard it, too, and peered up into the canopy of the redwoods until he spotted the bird.

"Look, it's a northern woodpecker!"

Emmy smiled. Two months ago, he'd studied the field guide to birds of northern California until he'd memorized them all, it seemed.

He'd since moved on to other field guides, but he still accurately identified every bird they came across, even the dead ones on the side of the road.

"I don't think he's going to come out and help," Max said. "He never comes outside."

"Let's wait and see," Emmy said quietly, not wanting Aidan to overhear them. "He's been busy writing a book."

"I'm going to write a book, too," Max said. "I want to write a treasure-hunting guide for Promise Lake."

"Do you think there's much more treasure buried around here?"

"There has to be. We found this today, and yesterday I found a bottle in the sand by the lake, and the day before that I found a metal tub."

"Sounds like you're becoming the treasure-hunting expert for the area. You'd be the person to write the book." This gave Emmy an idea. "Hey," she said casually, "Why don't you get your notebook from the cabin and start working on your guide while I wait for Aidan?"

Maybe if Max was gone, if the only person Aidan had to face was Emmy, he'd come out.

"But I want to see what's in the treasure chest!"

"I'll call you as soon as we've got the hinges off. We won't open it until you're here."

"But—"

"Go ahead, sweetie. Every good writer knows it's important to write while the ideas are fresh in your head."

He looked reluctant still, but with one more glance at the chest, he nodded. "Okay, but you promise you won't open it without me?"

"I promise."

He then took off at a run toward the guest cottage.

Emmy turned her attention back to the door. She tapped gently again. "Aidan? It's just me out here. Will you please come out and help?"

Silence.

She waited, and waited some more, feeling foolish that she thought she might be able to lure him outside.

Overhead, the woodpecker continued its ratta-tat-tatting. Emmy watched its flamboyant red head moving in the tree, and she remembered the time when she was a kid and she'd found the most thrilling treasure of her young life at the base of a bay tree—a tiny, perfect red feather, probably from the head of just such a wood-pecker.

She'd picked it up so gently, cradling it in her palm as if it were a delicate life she needed to protect. And it had seemed like something magical with its brilliant redness, so unlike the rest of the forest's palette of green and brown.

She'd kept the feather for years, tucked inside her nature journal. Like so many of the things she treasured in the past, she had no idea where it was anymore. That thought made her impossibly sad, much the same way seeing once-treasured objects from her marriage—a wedding portrait or a silk tapestry bought on a trip to China—made her ache for things forever lost.

Tears welled up in her eyes, and she blinked them away. She was prone to crying since the divorce. Not because she wanted her marriage back—she didn't—but because she now understood the stark reality of how changeable life was, how nothing was permanent, not even the love people tried to cement with vows.

She swallowed away the sadness that threatened to overtake her and turned her attention back to the chest. She too was wildly curious to know what was in it, and she wasn't going to make Max wait all day, over some misguided notion that she could lure Aidan outdoors.

So she picked up the chest and was about to head back to the cottage, when she heard the lock on the cabin click.

Finally, he opened the door.

HE WASN'T SURE what had made him want to do it. The lure of the chest, for sure, had played a part. But there was something more. Maybe the way the breeze had felt when he'd stood in the doorway, crisp and refreshing, but still a warm caress on his skin.

Maybe it was the light, the bright sunlight dancing on the leaves of the trees, so different from the dim existence inside the cabin.

For the first time since he'd come to Promise Lake, he ached to go outside.

And so, he'd opened the door. Emmy stood outside, holding the chest and looking at him as if waiting for the answer to a question.

Would he come out?

That was the question she wanted the answer to.

So he was the charity case she'd decided to take on, searching out a therapist for him and now trying herself to lure him out of his crazy exile with a mysterious chest that she could surely figure out how to open on her own.

But in spite of being aware of her machinations, some part of him wanted to go along with it.

"This wouldn't happen to be your chest, would it?" Emmy asked.

"Never seen it before in my life."

"The bulldozer turned it up while they were digging the foundation. I guess maybe it was buried by some member of my family."

"It looks pretty old."

"Yeah, it could have been there for decades."

"You have a screwdriver?"

Emmy nodded as she set the chest down next to the steps. Then she pulled the screwdriver from her pocket and bent to see if it would fit the screws in the hinges.

"Looks like it'll do the job," she said. "Would you mind giving me a hand? I've…got carpel tunnel syndrome, and I'm not supposed to do anything strenuous with my wrists."

"Oh."

His mouth went dry, and he could feel the telltale perspiration again, forming on his brow and beneath his shirt. But he hated Emmy seeing him like this, behaving like such a coward that even the benign world itself was too scary for him to face.

He wasn't going to let her believe he was a coward. He gripped the handle on the screen door that separated him from the outside, and he pushed the door open. Blinking in the bright sunlight, he forced himself to inhale the fresh air, to savor it. He wasn't going to let her believe he was a coward.

He wasn't.

He was going to do this thing. This simple thing that just involved putting one foot in front of the other, stepping out of the house and onto the steps.

He could do this.

He could.

He would.

Sweat dripping steadily down his ribcage, he forced his feet to move, as if learning for the first time how to walk. One step, then another, and another, and another. Down a step, then he sat.

His ass hit the wood of the top step hard, as if he'd lost control of his leg muscles, and he was seeing spots. The blinding light didn't help. He blinked and tried to focus on something close by—the chest—until he got control of his vision.

Then he realized Emmy was watching him, probably on alert to grab him if he pulled another Scarlett O'Hara. Once he could see straight, he looked up at her and forced himself to smile.

It probably looked more like a grimace, the way he was feeling, off kilter and on edge.

"It's okay, take your time."

"This is the first time I've been outside since…I don't know when."

It embarrassed him to admit it, but hell, she'd already seen him act like a lunatic on more than one occasion. What did he have left to lose?

"I can't think of a better day to change that," she said, smiling and looking up at the sky.

Aidan dared a glance upward, and he felt as if he were becoming unhinged from the earth, falling forward into the sky....

But he wasn't moving at all. He was just a little dizzy.

The sky was immense and far more blue and endless than it looked from inside the cabin through the window. The redwoods towered around them, tall, elegant giants, frozen in time. And the air smelled like trees and earth and summer, the best thing he'd ever smelled in his life.

It all made him sick with fear. And the fear made him loathe himself for not being able to enjoy this stunningly beautiful place.

"Are you feeling okay? Would you like a glass of water or anything?"

"No." No, he wasn't feeling okay, and no, he didn't want a glass of water.

He wanted to be immersed in water. He wanted to jump into the lake and swim until his muscles ached and his chest burned. He wanted to feel the water chill his body while the sun warmed his face. He wanted to splash and dive and play until he was so exhausted he couldn't move.

He stared out at Promise Lake, its surface broken by a million glistening ripples, and he hated himself for not being able to enjoy it like any normal living creature would.

Emmy placed the screwdriver next to him. She lifted the chest so that it sat between him and her, and Aidan took the tool in his hand.

He could do this. He wanted to know what was in the chest, and he could operate a screwdriver.

As he began working the screw out of the first hinge, the remaining chunks of dirt began to fall from the chest, and soon he had the screw out. The ancient hinge, having been in its proper place for countless years, didn't budge, but it would pop right off, he was sure, once the rest of the screws were out. Next he went to work on the second hinge.

Once he'd accomplished that task, Emmy placed her hands on top of the chest. "Wait," she said. "We can't open it until Max is here."

Aidan's gut wrenched. The kid? Here with him?

"Well, I'd better get back to work anyway," he said, starting to stand up.

"No, please. I'd like you to be here, too, to see what's inside." She placed a hand on his arm, and chills ran through him.

He looked down at her hand, and he gave up moving. Her pale skin looked golden against his, which hadn't seen the sun in far too long. She had skin that reminded him of the expensive china dolls his grandmother collected, dolls he'd stared at as a kid, half bored by them and half fascinated by how eerily real they looked.

He was struck by a flash of memory, of lying with Emmy some time during college, probably on a lazy Sunday morning, and watching her hand resting on him as she slept, and being filled by the ridiculous kind of all-encompassing love that only naive first lovers could feel.

Since then he'd lived. He'd had his heart broken.

He'd seen death and destruction of the most senseless kinds. He'd never be able to feel that way again.

Emmy, reading his expression, pulled her hand away. "Please," she said. "Just stay here a bit longer. The sun is good for you. You need the vitamin D."

He said nothing, but he didn't move, either.

"Max!" she called toward the cottage. "We're ready to open the chest now!"

There was some movement in the cottage's front window. The kid had probably been watching the whole time, waiting for his chance to come out and see the hidden treasures. In a flash, Max burst through the door and came running across the stone path.

Aidan could understand the kid's excitement. Hell, he'd been intrigued enough to set foot outside.

The kid was barefoot and bare-chested, wearing only an old faded pair of orange swim trunks. He stopped at the bottom step and peered up at Aidan warily.

"Is it your treasure chest?" he asked.

Aidan shook his head. "Nope."

Max looked as if he didn't quite believe him. Well, he'd see soon enough. Aidan wasn't a pirate, and this old chest wasn't filled with booty. It was probably a bunch of old papers, something someone hadn't wanted found but hadn't wanted to destroy either.

"Max, I'm going to open the chest first and make sure there's nothing bad in it, okay? Then I'll let you see inside," Emmy said.

"But I wanna open it!"

"There's a small chance something scary could be in here."

"So what? I don't care."

Emmy sighed. "Just stay back for a second."

She bent and lifted the lid. As she peered inside, her expression changed from apprehensive to curious. "It's okay," she said to Max. "You can open it."

The kid beamed and scurried up the steps to the chest. He grabbed the lid in his scrawny hands and opened it. Then they all stared inside.

The space inside the chest was about a foot deep and two feet wide, and the contents were wrapped with tissue paper that had yellowed with age. The edges of a bundle of letters could be seen, along with a dried rose that lay on top of the whole bundle.

Emmy gently picked up the rose and set it aside, then she pushed the tissue paper out of the way to reveal all of the contents. Besides the letters, there was a gold necklace, a small wooden box shaped like a heart, a piece of blue sea glass and some more things underneath that Aidan couldn't see.

"What is all this stuff?" Max said, going for the sea glass.

"It looks like someone's special treasures that they didn't want anyone to take from them."

"But not a pirate's treasure?"

"No, sweetie. I don't think so," Emmy said gently.

Aidan's throat tightened at the way she talked to her son. He had never seen this side of her before. She'd always been a kind person overall, but she'd also been a spoiled princess when he'd loved her. He'd fallen for her in spite of the way she thought the world revolved around her, and the way she had only been interested in other people's needs when it suited her.

Perhaps age and motherhood had matured her, brought out a maternal side she'd been sorely lacking in her younger years.

Either way, he didn't really give a damn.

Digging through the contents of the chest again, Emmy paused. Aidan watched as her face drained of color. She carefully picked up the object that had stopped her in her tracks. It was a small red leather journal, decorated with a baroque design, and it looked oddly familiar.

Aidan didn't understand why until she opened it, her hands shaking, and gasped. She turned the open page so that he could see it. The first line was in his own handwriting and read: For Emmaline Victoria Van Amsted.

The rest of the page was in his handwriting, too, but he didn't need to read it to know what it said. It was a poem he'd written for Emmy all those years ago, a poem he still knew by heart.

The very thought of you
Sends me spinning
You the kite soaring high
I the spool of string
Clinging
Trailing after

Holding you to this earth
When you were made to fly above.

The journal had been a gift from him to her, for her
twentieth birthday. They'd passed it back and forth
between themselves, writing love notes or silly limer-
icks or passionate poems or whatever popped into their
heads. They'd pasted in ticket stubs and favorite snap-
shots and odd bits of memories from their life together.

It sometimes amazed him to think back to that time
and remember that he'd once been so unabashedly
romantic. He felt as if where once his soul had been
blooming full of love and idealism, now there dwelled
a hardened little black acorn, scorched and lifeless.

On their last trip here to Promise Lake together, the
journal had gone missing, never to be seen again, and
Emmy had been heartbroken by its loss.

So had Aidan.

His vision went blurry, but not before he caught
sight of tears streaming down Emmy's cheeks.

"How did this—"

She didn't need to finish the question. He wondered
the same thing, of course.

He took a few deep breaths and tried to exhale the
mounting tension in his gut. Tried to keep his head
calm and clear, free of panic or misplaced emotions he
didn't want to feel.

Maybe the rest of the contents would offer some explanation of how the journal had gotten into the chest.
He bent and pushed aside the tissue paper himself,

watching as Max rummaged through the remaining contents, oblivious to the drama that had just played out over the journal. He was more concerned with finding some booty that hadn't been unearthed yet.

Aidan took the bundle of letters and examined the address on the first one. It was addressed in a formal, meticulous script to someone named Leticia Van Amsted, and the mailing address was here at the lake cabin. The return address was a W. Elliot, on Scott Street in San Francisco. And the postmark date, barely legible, was October 10, 1945.

Someone had buried letters from over fifty years ago, with a journal of theirs that had disappeared only twelve years ago?

It didn't make any sense.

"Whose are those?" Emmy asked.

"They're addressed to a Leticia Van Amsted."

"Oh," she said, frowning. "That's my great-aunt."

Emmy paled again. Aidan watched confusion play on her face, until he couldn't take looking at her anymore.

He wanted to kiss her. He wanted more than anything on this godforsaken earth to kiss her and feel the same love he'd felt when he'd picked out the journal she was holding and poured all his stupid young passion into it.

No. He recalled their recent kiss, right after she'd arrived at the cabin, and he knew he couldn't do that again. He couldn't bear to feel her respond to him then pull away. It was like arriving in heaven for a moment only to be told that there'd been a mistake—you were actually going to hell.

Maybe that was a bit of an overblown description, but his feelings for Emmy—both the good and the bad ones—had always been epic.

"Probably somebody gathered up a bunch of stuff that had been lying around in the cabin and—"

"And buried it in the forest? Why would anyone do that?"

He looked at the letters in his hand. "I don't know."

"And *who* would have done it? Certainly not my father, but he's owned this place ever since my great-aunt died in the late forties and he inherited it."

Aidan puzzled over that one for a moment. "Were there any caretakers or maids hired to keep the place up when no one was here?"

Emmy shrugged. "I imagine so, but why would they bury a bunch of our family's personal belongings in a chest in the woods?"

"Maybe the ghost did it," Max said matter-of-factly, as if it was such an obvious truth they were stupid not to have thought of it. "Isn't the ghost really Aunt Leticia?"

"How do you know about that?" Emmy asked.

"My cousin told me."

Emmy sighed. "I don't believe in ghosts, honey. There's no proof they really exist."

"But what about that teacup?"

"What?"

"The teacup that keeps moving out of the cabinet."

Emmy stared at him as if he'd just said something disturbing. "The one with the pink roses on it?"

"Yeah. Every time you put it away, it ends up back on the windowsill."

"I thought you were doing that for a science experiment or something."

Max shook his head. "Nuh-uh."

"Then…how is it getting there? Tell me the truth, Max. This is not a time for joking, okay?"

"I swear! I'm not moving it."

A chill went up Aidan's spine. He hadn't seen any evidence of a supernatural presence during his time in the cabin, but he'd had his own mental instability to deal with. Maybe he simply hadn't noticed.

No, that was crazy talk. There were no ghosts here, other than the ones that haunted him from within.

Emmy was shaking her head, looking distressed and puzzled. "I—I'm sure there's a logical explanation, Max. There are no such things as ghosts."

The kid looked as though he didn't believe a thing his mother was saying, but he didn't argue. He dug into the chest again, rummaged around, and pulled out a gold ring.

"Look," he said. "There really is treasure in here. Maybe some pirates broke into the cabin and took the stuff they liked and buried it in the woods."

"That's about as good an explanation as any I can think of," Emmy said, staring at the journal again and shaking her head. "Pirates."

Aidan's gaze dropped to her torso, encased in a pink

cotton tank top that stretched over her curves, and his groin stirred at the sight of her lush cleavage. He'd always loved her chest, but now it was an entirely different world from the one he'd known. She had full curves where she'd once been a bit too thin, and it made him wonder again how different she'd be in ways he couldn't see by looking at her.

Was she more experienced and responsive in bed now? More confident? More uninhibited?

He felt himself growing hard. What the hell was he doing? Torturing himself? Hadn't he had enough of that for one lifetime?

Apparently not.

The worst thing about surviving any long-term trauma, Aidan suspected, was the habit it formed, the lingering impulse to experience the kinds of pain that felt like normal life to someone who didn't know any better.

It made him understand why people sought out abusive relationships after growing up abused.

If he had a saving grace though, it was that deep down, he didn't want his months as a hostage to define who he was for the rest of his life.

He was still trying to escape his captivity.

Forcing his mind off Emmy brought him back to reality. And his attention turned to the fact that he was still outside—with two other people, no less. When he wasn't thinking about it, he wasn't freaking out about it.

But now… He felt panic stirring in his gut, so he

tricked himself by turning his attention back to the letters he was still holding. Emmy had set aside the journal and was reading the inscription in the ring Max had found.

"To LV, with all my heart," she read aloud.

Aidan opened the first letter in the stack. The old paper was delicate, but not crumbling. It had yellowed, and was darker around the edges, but the dark-blue ink was still perfectly legible.

He began reading.

My dearest Leticia,

How long have I ached to be near you? I watch you from afar each day, and I cannot bear to think that soon the summer will be here, and I will be without even the sight of you for three long, tedious months. And so I have set the task upon myself to tell you how I feel.

AIDAN STOPPED at the second paragraph. He wasn't in the mood to read about unrequited love—or any other kind, for that matter. He didn't need to know about some poor sap who'd gotten his heart broken by another Van Amsted woman. That was a subject he'd already become an expert on.

He tucked the letter in its envelope, then tucked the envelope back under the twine that held the bundle of letters together, and he dropped the whole lot back into the chest.

"This stuff," Emmy said, "except for the journal, it

seems to be mostly Great-Aunt Leticia's. I just don't get it."

Aidan's mood turned dark. This Technicolor perfect day... This ridiculously pretty setting... Emmy standing before him looking like a portrait of good health and beauty, of grown-up sexual vitality... This sickeningly cute kid with his brain that was too damn big for his body...

It all seemed to be conspiring against him, mocking him for being such a head case, laughing at his inability to participate in life.

"Yeah well, I'd love to sit here and help you sort out your family ghost stories, but I've got work to do," he said and stood.

Before they could protest, he stomped into the cabin and slammed the door. And there, alone in the cool, dark room, away from the sunlight and the trees and Emmy, he was weighed down by a sadness so heavy, he feared it might crush him if he didn't escape it soon.

CHAPTER SIX

We were held hostage for two months and five days, but I'd only been a hostage for a few hours when I started considering how we would escape. Getting myself and my fellow soldiers out alive occupied my every waking thought, and some of my dreaming ones, for that entire two months. I noted which guards were less vigilant, which had a lazy air about them or a tendency to leave the door open upon entering the room. I mentally noted the sounds I could hear through the windows, trying desperately to orient myself to where I was and where I might go when we escaped.

From *Through a Soldier's Eyes*
by Aidan Caldwell

EMMY HAD maybe fifteen minutes of peace and quiet before Max would get bored watching the construction work and come in to bug her again about going swimming. Capable as he was of entertaining himself, she knew he missed having other kids to interact with more and more as the quiet days beside the lake ticked by. And much as she looked forward to him going to day camp so she could have more work time, she also knew she'd have a hard time letting him go away all day. She had a tendency to cling to him a bit too much lately.

She hurried to pack a beach bag with towels, sun block and other necessities, then set it by the door.

Now, where had she put her swimsuit?

She found it hanging in the bathroom, barely damp from their swim the day before.

Emmy could feel the presence of the chest no matter what she was doing. As she undressed, she tried to ignore it. She found herself casting apprehensive glances at it every so often—when she was working, or cleaning up, or making the bed or getting dressed.

She'd been afraid to open it up again since bringing it into the cottage. She hadn't wanted to start reading the journal, rekindling old feelings best laid to rest, or even remembering the things she and Aidan had written to each other. Back when they were together, she'd considered his frivolous romanticism a sweet but silly trait to be endured, and she'd indulged it by going along with it most of the time.

But now that she'd experienced the world away from Aidan, she understood just how rare he was in that regard. How rare it was to find a man comfortable enough with his softer emotions to express his love for her in such an open and honest way. She didn't want to get sucked back into feelings that were inappropriate in her current life.

She was no longer the selfish coed who'd fallen for Aidan. She was a grown woman who couldn't afford the energy or emotional fallout that could come along with getting involved in the sort of intense relationship Aidan couldn't help but have. She had to consider her own needs, and Max's, and how it took all she had just to keep him cared for and get her work done every day. Where was there room for any man, let alone one so much bigger than life as Aidan?

There wasn't any room. Nor did she even have the energy to try to fit him in.

And it wasn't only the journal she and Aidan had shared that kept her away from the chest. She'd even been afraid to take a closer look at the other contents. That someone had deliberately gathered then buried their treasures suggested those items contained secrets and revelations that Emmy wasn't prepared to face at the moment. She knew she'd need to do it sooner or later, but with all the stressors in her life right now, she'd simply set the chest aside to deal with another day.

Max, for his part, was thrilled with the discovery of the chest. It fueled his imagination, and he'd spent the rest of the day after finding it furiously working on his treasure-hunting guide.

Which was, essentially, a bunch of childish drawings and incomprehensible maps of the forest and lake, along with his very rudimentary efforts at writing. As a reader, he was extremely gifted, but he still had the fine motor skills of a six-year-old, and the handwriting to match. Also, while his reading comprehension vocabulary was high, that didn't always translate into his being able to spell words accurately as he wrote.

"Follow the trail to the big sequoia tree by the water" became, "Falo the trayl to the big sakoya tree by the water," and so forth. It might not have been all that easy to read, but for a kid his age, it was still pretty impressive.

In only a day's time, he'd completed most of his text and drawings and had moved on to adding color to the pictures.

Undressed now, Emmy caught a glimpse of herself in the long mirror on the back of the bathroom door. Since having Max she'd rarely spent time gazing at herself in mirrors, inspecting the landscape of her body for flaws the way she had in her pre-kid days.

And since the divorce, she'd nearly stopped thinking of herself as a sexual being. So she was surprised to see this side-angle view of herself, looking like a real, live, flesh-and-blood woman who should and did have sexual needs.

She trailed a hand gently up her stomach, causing goose flesh to dot her skin, and felt her insides go liquid at the sensation of it.

It had been too long since she'd been touched— really touched—by a man. The massage her mother had bought her last month didn't count, since that guy was being paid to touch her.

The afternoon light pouring through the window cast a soft, yellow light on her skin that flattered her coloring and made her look like a painting she'd seen somewhere. A portrait of a normal woman, no other-worldly beauty, just a woman like her, who was still, in her naked imperfection, beautiful.

She thought of Aidan in the cabin next door, and the way he'd kissed her that first day, the way she'd kissed him back so eagerly, and the way her body had ached just as it did now. She thought of how they'd made love years ago, so often in a frenzy of never getting enough. They were not the most skilled lovers in the world back then, but they'd made up for it with enthusiasm.

No sooner had her thoughts strayed to sex than from outside the cottage Max called, "Mommy! Hurry up, I want to go!"

Emmy sighed at his timing, grabbed her swimsuit and dashed for the bathroom. Before she closed the bathroom door, she called out to Max, "I'll be out in just a minute."

She resigned herself to sexual frustration yet again, as she put on the swimsuit, a baby-blue one-piece tank-style suit that had seemed lovely and refined on the store rack, but now that she looked at herself in the mirror in it, she saw it for the matronly mommy suit it was.

She wanted a bikini, something skimpy and bohemian, maybe with some little wooden beads and ties at the hips. She wanted to wear it proudly, unafraid of revealing her body's grown-up curves, to splash in the lake with her son looking like her own woman, not just like someone else's mom.

She resolved to go into town in the morning and find

such a suit, as she left the cottage and met up with Max on the stone path toward the lake.

It wasn't that she didn't love being a mother. She did. But in the days before her divorce she'd seen how she'd sacrificed herself and how she might lose herself completely—to her work, to her child, to her husband or to any of the big demands life made on her. That realization, coupled with Steven's infidelity and their crumbling relationship, led to her vow to live more authentically. And while she still had a way to go, she was being more true to herself. The bikini was one more step.

As they walked, Max talked nonstop about another map he'd thought to add to his treasure-hunting book, and Emmy, though she wanted to be good and pay attention, found her mind wandering.

Her body was still tense with sexual frustration. And she found herself aware of the way she was moving, of the way her body bounced and felt heavy in certain places. She felt as if she were awakening from a deep sleep, and her primary awareness upon waking was of herself as a sexual being.

She had needs, and she'd been ignoring them for too long.

A few men had tried to flirt with her since she'd come to town. There was Jerry Lawson, the town mayor, whom she'd bumped into in the coffee house a few days ago. She'd studiously ignored his efforts to charm her.

Could she be attracted to Jerry? Even for a night?

He was a nice enough guy, she supposed, but he had a certain smarmy quality that turned her off. No, Jerry definitely wasn't going to do it for her.

They arrived at the lake's edge, and as Emmy spread out a towel on the sand, Max splashed right into the water, squealing at the cold but not letting it stop him for a second.

Why did adults so often lose the ability to do that, to dive right in and bear the shock of entry to enjoy a good thing?

She watched him as she sat on the towel and began slathering on sunscreen. She'd already put some on Max before he'd gone out to play for the day, but in spite of diligent applications, his skin was turning bronze from being outside every day. He had her complexion, but with a touch of his father's, too—so that he was less susceptible to burning than she was.

Max, already becoming a confident swimmer, dove down under the water and came up with a rock. He hauled it to the shore and sat hunched over it, probably examining it for gold flecks. He frequently asked when they'd get to go panning for gold in the gold country— ever since one of his friends in San Francisco had told him about a similar trip his family had done.

Emmy wondered where Max got his interest in finding treasure. It certainly hadn't come from her. Maybe it was one of those natural kid things, or maybe it was because he'd watched *Pirates of the Caribbean* at his grandfather's house a few months ago. But some part of her worried that maybe it was an unhealthy interest. Maybe he was responding to the instability in his life by wanting to find some quick-fix solution, such as a treasure chest full of riches.

Okay, she was probably being way too neurotic there.

Still, she made a mental note to find a child therapist in the area and get Max an appointment, just to be sure he had a safe place to talk about any post-divorce anxiety he might be having.

His father hadn't called Max since leaving on the trip to Tibet, but Max asked about him perhaps once a day. And he frequently looked up Tibet on his world map, sometimes staring at the country for fifteen minutes or more, tracing his fingers around its zig-zaggy border and trying to pronounce the names of its towns and counties.

The sight of him staring at the map as if he might find his father there never failed to break her heart a little bit more.

"Mommy," he might say, "what is *Aba?*"

And Emmy would bring him to her computer to search for the city on the Internet with him so they could read about it and look at pictures.

Now that they had a reliable Internet connection via Aidan's unsecured wireless network, she'd been resisting showing Max Google Earth, because she so often needed her computer free for work, and she was afraid he'd become obsessed with looking up his father on the interactive maps. But, she realized, he would love it so much, she was cheating him by not letting him use the site. So she resolved that she would show him tonight.

"Hey, little man, whatcha got there?" she heard a voice call out from the north end of the beach, where a path from the road gave the public access to this secluded part of the lakeshore—or at least it gave access to the few people who knew about the path.

She looked and saw a man she didn't recognize, tall and good-looking, strolling toward them. He had shoulder-length wavy blond hair and an athletic build of the type that usually came from working and playing outdoors rather than any deliberate effort to get buff. He was bare-chested and tan, with a pair of navy swim trunks hanging low on his narrow hips.

Emmy found herself sucking in her stomach and feeling conscious of how frumpy and conservative she probably looked in her mom-style swimsuit.

Then she rolled her eyes at herself and made a mental note not to be such an idiot.

The man smiled and nodded at her. He wasn't quite as good-looking as Aidan, but he was certainly easy on the eyes. When he knelt next to Max and appeared interested in Max's rock, Emmy gave herself a mental slap on the head for even holding Aidan up as a measure of anything.

"It's a piece of granite," Max offered to the man.

"Nice. You'll find a lot of that around here, you know. What's your name?"

"Max."

"I'm Devan. Nice to meet you, Max."

He held out his hand for the boy to shake, but Max only looked at it warily.

"Right on, little man. Good idea not to trust weirdos like me."

Max tossed the rock aside, no longer interested in it, and ran to the water without saying another word. He'd never been all that interested in socializing with grown-ups, in spite of his intelligence...or maybe because of it.

"Hi," Devan said to Emmy now. "You guys here visiting?"

"Actually no," Emmy said. "We've just moved here permanently."

"Excellent. If you need any information about the area—"

"I spent my summers here growing up," Emmy said, ridiculously wanting to set herself apart from the once-in-a-while tourists. Being a summer resident wasn't much better in the eyes of the locals, but it did have a bit of added cache.

Why did she even care? For all she knew, this guy was a tourist himself. Except, well, he had the slightly grungy, hippied-out look of a true local. And she vaguely recognized him now that she had a close-up view, though she wasn't sure from where.

He sat on the sand next to her and gazed out at the lake.

"What's your family name? Maybe I know some of your folks."

"Van Amsted."

"Oh, whoa, really? Like Drew Van Amsted?"

"He's my little brother."

Devan smiled then. "Yeah, I remember you guys. I used to play soccer with Drew in the summers over at Sequoia Park."

"You look vaguely familiar. Maybe I saw you guys together sometime."

He grinned. "I'm sure I'd remember if I'd seen a girl as gorgeous as you around."

Emmy was not so naive that she could mistake a sentence referring to her as both a girl and gorgeous as anything but a blatant come-on.

But this guy Devan...if he'd been hanging out with Drew, he was definitely younger than her. And judging by the lack of lines on his face, she imagined quite a bit younger. Surely he wasn't looking at her as a sexual prospect. She hadn't been mistaken for under thirty, since...well, since she'd been under thirty.

She ignored his compliment. "I'm probably six or eight years older than you. That's why you don't remember me."

"Get out of here. What're you? Like twenty-five, twenty-six?"

Emmy laughed. "Don't be ridiculous. I'm thirty-five."

As soon as the words exited her mouth, she wondered if she should have kept the fact to herself. Would he totally lose interest now?

She didn't know anything about this guy, but she didn't want to shut down this fun little flirtation before it had even gotten started.

Aidan invaded her thoughts again. He was probably

sitting in his cabin, glaring at his computer right now. And he had good reason to glare, given the trauma he'd been through. She wondered if Devan had ever done anything that required risking his life for the greater good.

"Well, you do the age of thirty-five proud, if you don't mind my saying so."

She caught his gaze dropping to her chest, and she found herself happy to be stared at there for once. She glanced down and saw that her nipples were hard beneath her swimsuit, and the suit itself was light enough in color that the dark skin of her nipples actually showed through faintly. Yet another flaw in this suit that she'd failed to notice at the store.

Oh well, she supposed there were worse things he could be seeing right now.

"So where'd you and your husband move from?"

He was definitely interested. Even after hearing her age, and getting a full-on inspection of her in her granny suit. Doubtful he'd go fishing with the "your husband" phrase otherwise.

Amazing.

"Actually it's just me and my son. I'm divorced from his father."

"He's a cute kid," Devan added. "I've got a five-year-old girl myself. I'm not with her mother anymore, but I've got custody of her half the time. Maybe we could get them together for a play date sometime."

Oh, the old playdate-that's-actually-a-grown-up-date maneuver. Smooth.

She felt a tiny bit awkward hanging out with a man—a potential love interest, even?—with Max present, too. She'd never done that before. The last time she'd spent a day with Max and another man, it had been his father, and the thought created a dull, momentary ache in her belly.

She would not let those thoughts ruin this perfectly lovely day. Instead, she forced her mind back to the present and Devan's offer.

"Sure, that would be great. Max doesn't know any kids his age here yet. What's your daughter's name?"

"Zoe. I'm actually picking her up tomorrow afternoon, and I'll have her for the weekend, if you guys are going to be around."

"We will be," Emmy said, trying her best to sound casual. "Maybe we'll bump into you at the festival tomorrow."

"I'll be sure to keep an eye out for you."

It struck Emmy as odd that the times she'd been in the presence of both Max and Aidan, she didn't feel the same sense of tense awkwardness she felt now, with Devan. Being with Aidan felt like slipping back into a favorite pair of jeans—he just fit.

No.

He didn't, and it was stupid of her to think that way. He was more like an old destructive habit—smoking, or drinking—that she'd done to excess in the past and now had to be diligent against if she wanted to take care of herself.

Because with him, she'd been out of control, impulsive, too passionate, too consumed by his energy—none of the things she could afford to be as a mother. She had to think of Max first now. Always. And he needed a stable, calm, responsible mother. She couldn't afford to lose herself to a man any more than she could to motherhood, or to any of the other roles she played in life.

Just as there was a delicate balance between being a good mother and holding onto her sense of self separate from motherhood, there was the same balance necessary between having a love relationship and becoming engulfed by the flames of it. Aidan had already proven once that he could engulf her.

Right now, she had a perfectly nice guy sitting next to her, and the last thing she should have been doing was comparing him to Aidan.

"If you come to this beach again, we live in the house on the other side right back there," Emmy said, pointing through the trees at the cottage.

"Oh right, your family property. I remember visiting your brother at that place when we were kids."

"We're living in the guest cottage behind the main house, so if you're coming to the beach, feel free to knock on our door and see if we're around."

"Sure," he said, smiling. "I'll do that."

Emmy tried not to grin too widely. She wasn't used to flirting with men anymore. She closed her eyes and tilted her head toward the sky.

"I think I'm going to cool off in the water," Devan said and stood.

The sun warmed Emmy's skin to the point of stinging, a sensation she'd always loved in spite of being afraid of sunburn. She didn't want to get in the water yet—she'd wait until she was drenched in sweat and couldn't take the heat any longer. She lay back on the towel, still aware of the humming in her body.

Nearby, Max was splashing in the water, and she could hear Devan joking around with him.

She needed a man. Well, no. That sounded awful. She didn't *need a man*. She needed physical intimacy. And perhaps a little emotional intimacy. Maybe some grown-up conversation, or even some clever pillow talk would be fine with her.

Okay, she needed to get laid, pure and simple.

Casting a lingering glance at Devan as he stood with his back to her, waist-deep in the water, she tried to picture herself getting it on with him. He was young and gorgeous and was probably blessed with incredible stamina.

The image didn't create any wild frenzy of desire in her, but there were definitely stirrings of…something. The lack of frenzied feelings was probably because she needed to get to know a guy before she really knew if she was attracted to him.

She could certainly do worse than getting to know Devan.

Maybe… Maybe he could be the one to end her long sexual drought.

An image of Aidan invaded her thoughts, and she tried to banish it, but it wouldn't go away. Aidan, that unwanted ghost from her past. Why had he come back into her life now, when she was trying to get a fresh start?

Perhaps the answer to that question was obvious, but she didn't want to ponder it. Her therapist in San Francisco would have said she had unfinished business with him, and she would have been right.

That didn't make the business any easier to finish, or her desire for him any more appropriate, given the circumstances.

CHAPTER SEVEN

Pain, when endured over many hours' time, becomes an exercise much like meditation. There is a constant training of the mind back toward a place of not responding. During the first hour or so of torture, the mind must adjust to the reality of the pain, the constant presence of it, and once that mental adjustment has been made, it's easier to disassociate oneself from the experience. I did not have any of the information our captors wanted from us, but it took them many hours to figure that out.

From *Through a Soldier's Eyes*
by Aidan Caldwell

SATURDAY MORNING, Aidan felt hung-over from an especially crappy night's sleep. He'd had a particularly vivid nightmare that he'd never quite gotten out of his head, and now he caught himself lying in bed, staring out the window again. It afforded him a view of the guest cottage—or more importantly, Emmy's comings and goings from it—and staring at it too much made him feel like a pathetic stalker.

Especially when he couldn't even get out of bed to do his stalking.

He had tried keeping all the blinds closed, so that he wouldn't be tortured by the sight of Emmy and her kid all day long. But it didn't help, because he could still hear them, and even when he couldn't, he still knew they were there.

Also, sitting in the cabin all day with no natural light was a recipe for insanity. Even he knew that he needed the little bit of light he was getting while staying indoors all the time.

So he kept the blinds open, and he obsessed over looking out the window.

He got up and went to the bathroom, then paced out of the bedroom to the kitchen, where he intended to make a cup of coffee, until he realized he'd forgotten to request more coffee in his last bag of groceries. He stared dumbfounded into the cabinet where the fresh package of coffee should have been, but instead, there was only an empty space.

Coffee. How could he have forgotten? He didn't function without it, especially not since he'd started sleeping so badly.

He. Needed. Coffee. Right. *Now.*

Like a true addict, his heart started racing as he realized the supply of his chosen drug was gone. His mouth went dry, and he broke into a cold sweat. The grocery bag he'd unloaded yesterday afternoon still sat on the counter, empty now, but he went to it and stared into it again as if a half pound of French roast might appear out of thin air.

He went to the refrigerator next, where he sometimes kept open packages of coffee to keep them from going stale, but as he'd known, there was none there either. His hands shook as he moved aside milk and orange juice cartons.

He slammed the refrigerator door and opened the coffeemaker to see if he'd left any used grounds in the filter from yesterday. None. It had been cleaned out.

Damn it. Damn it, damn it, damn it.

He'd have to place another delivery order. But it was Saturday. No grocery deliveries on Saturday.

Then he'd have to ask Emmy for coffee. Which would mean leaving the house, unless he could catch her on her way out. Then he remembered, she might be gone all day if he didn't catch her soon.

Although Aidan didn't read the local paper—or any newspaper these days, for that matter—he knew today was the first day of the annual town festival, thanks to a flyer the grocery store had stuck in his bag of groceries. And surely Emmy would be going to it.

He remembered going to that very same festival with Emmy during their college days. They'd drunk beer until their heads swam and danced barefoot on the grass to a live band and had a great time.

He could not recognize that carefree, crazy-in-love version of himself anymore.

He was, at best, a ghost of that person.

Back in the bedroom again, his body still panicking over the lack of coffee in the house, he could see through the window that Emmy was outside now. She sat in a lawn chair, not looking like she would be hurrying off to the festival at any moment. So he had time.

Except, well, his body wanted coffee now, not however long from now it took for him to work up the courage to open the door and call out her name, and for her to go to the store and bring back the—

His gut wrenched at the realization of what he'd be asking her to do. Get in her car with her kid, drive the ten minutes into town, buy him some coffee, and then drive it back to him. As soon as possible.

Could he really ask someone—particularly this woman he'd been estranged from for most of his adult life—to do him such a pathetic favor? All because he was too much of a head case to leave his own house?

His pride screamed, hell no. He'd already humiliated himself in front of her too many times. He couldn't bear another insult.

Standing near the window now, he watched transfixed as he took note of her nearly naked body in the lawn chair. She was wearing a crocheted red bikini, like an X-rated doily, and she looked insanely hot in it. He'd seen her the day before in a modest blue tank suit that, while it wasn't the sexiest thing he'd ever seen, did show off her curves nicely. But now she had this other suit on as she sat outside in the sun reading a magazine and she looked better than he'd ever seen her in her life.

The kid was playing with the water hose's sprinkler nozzle, watering himself and the plants in the garden, but every so often he'd turn the hose on his mother and give her a good soaking. She'd squeal and tell him to stop, and he would, but soon enough he'd be doing it again.

Finally, fed up, she set the magazine aside and started chasing him. Aidan's gaze followed her hungrily around the garden as she ran, her womanly body firm but swaying deliciously as she moved.

When she caught the kid, she grabbed the hose and turned it on him until he was soaked and giggling uncontrollably, then she gave him a squeeze and set him free. He ran off, shaking like a wet dog, toward the redwoods.

Emmy went to the side of the cottage to turn off the faucet, then grabbed a towel from her chair and dried off as she watched her son. Aidan's gaze lingered a bit too long on the lovely curves of her ass, barely concealed in the low-cut bikini bottom, until he could feel himself getting hard. Pretty soon he was going to go insane from sexual frustration, if the agoraphobia didn't get him first.

Okay, think. If he couldn't ask Emmy for help, then what was he going to do? Maybe he could find out if she happened to be going to the store anyway....

No, that was as pathetic as asking her outright for help.

Maybe she had some coffee that he could borrow. He felt stupid for not having thought of it in the first place. Of course. Everyone kept coffee around.

So he simply had to open the door and ask her.

Open the door.

And ask her.

Aidan glared at the door that stood between them, then looked away from it. Why did the simplest things have to be so difficult?

The kid came wandering back now that his mother was no longer in possession of the water hose. He got interested in something on the ground, and Aidan heard Emmy say to him, "Ten more minutes, Max. Then we have to get ready to go to the festival."

Ten more minutes—that was how long he had to open the door, and talk to her. It should not have seemed so damn impossible.

Aidan tried to swallow the dryness in his mouth, then realized he needed a drink of water. He went to the kitchen, tried to down a glass of tap water, but his stomach was too knotted with tension to accept more than a small sip.

Sighing at his own idiocy, he closed his eyes and leaned against the kitchen counter. He told himself to think calming thoughts, and the first image that came to his mind was the canopy of trees outside the cabin.

The very environment he was so afraid to step into.

He imagined the crystalline blue sky, the warm breeze, the calls of the birds, and he knew he had to go out there. His last shred of self-respect depended upon it.

So before he could freak out, he walked straight to the back door and unlocked it, swung it open and forced his feet to propel him onto the steps.

Emmy looked up from her magazine, startled to see

him, while Max scampered off into the woods chasing a butterfly, oblivious to the adult drama playing out nearby.

"Hi," she said tentatively.

Aidan forced his mouth open and croaked out a greeting.

"Gorgeous day, huh?" she said, setting her magazine aside.

"I—I need some coffee," he said dumbly.

Way to save his pride—by sounding like an idiot.

"Excuse me?"

He couldn't stand here frozen like this. He had to move. Now.

One foot in front of the other, down a step, and another, then forward, across the stone path, one foot, and the other. One foot, and the other.

And there he was standing next to Emmy's chair. A second one faced hers, presumably set up for the kid. Aidan sat on it and forced himself to breathe.

Emmy seemed to be struggling over whether to comment on his emergence from the cabin. In the end, she opted not to. She just smiled gently at him instead, as if he were the guy with the knife who'd just escaped the mental institution.

"Did you say you need *coffee?*" she asked.

He nodded, hearing exactly how ridiculous he sounded. He closed his eyes so that he could savor the feel of the breeze against his skin. Even the sun, already hot for so early in the day, felt good burning his face.

"I don't have any, I'm sorry."

"What?" Aidan opened his eyes again and looked at her as disappointment settled in.

"I don't drink coffee anymore."

"But…"

"You came all the way out here to ask me for a cup of coffee?"

"I was hoping to borrow some from you. I'm all out, and I can't write without it."

"Oh, well, I wish I could help."

"I could give you some money if you don't mind stopping at the store for some."

She looked at him oddly, but finally said, "Sure. I'll be in town again later today—I already went in this morning to pick up some milk and stuff. Too bad you didn't ask me first thing."

"Later? How much later?"

She shrugged. "We're leaving soon but I'll probably be there most of the day."

Okay, so that's what he'd have to do. He'd have to somehow survive the day without coffee until she got back. He could do that, couldn't he?

Maybe.

Maybe not.

"It's really great you're getting outside a little," Emmy said.

"Yeah, I guess."

He scowled out at the lake, almost hating it for being so beautiful. It tormented him and made his confinement seem all the more ridiculous. But no one really understood. Aidan wasn't even sure he understood.

It wasn't the first time something beautiful had made him angry. It was as if places like this made a mockery of the ugliness he'd seen in Sudan, just by their existence on the planet. How could such horror and such beauty exist simultaneously on the same earth?

Why did it feel like horror could decimate beauty, but never the other way around?

He'd tried to work through those questions in his book, but the answers eluded him. Whenever he got close to the truth, he was tormented by the simplicity of it just out of his reach.

"Did you get a chance to call that therapist?"

"No." He didn't want to be reminded either that Emmy was a witness to his lunacy, that she'd felt compelled to seek out mental treatment options for him.

Aidan started to stand, to retreat to the cabin again, but Emmy reached out and placed a hand on his where he held onto the arm of the chair.

"Please don't go," she said. "I'm sorry if I brought up a touchy subject."

He would have ignored her except that the contact of her hand on his sent a shock wave through him, and he had no choice but to sit back down. He thought of the way it had felt to kiss her, and he wanted badly to take her to his cabin and touch and kiss and savor every inch of her, to bury himself safe, deep and warm inside of her until they both forgot about the painful ugliness and beauty of the outside world.

Instead, he expelled a ragged sigh.

"One more thing, and don't answer me right away,

just think about it. I could make an appointment for you, for the therapist to come here, I mean."

Her hand was still covering his. He stared at it, long and delicate, the skin just beginning to show the slightest wrinkling. There, around the knuckles, was the physical evidence of time passing, of Emmy, like him, growing older every day and slowly, slowly, slipping away from life on this earth.

Was this how he was going to spend the precious little time they had? Locked away in a dark cabin, haunted by ghosts of the past? When he had a very real life here left to live?

Here was Emmy, her hand on his, older now than when he first loved her. And maybe she was here for a reason, here so that they could have a chance to undo mistakes of the past, or perhaps here to remind him that he shouldn't waste this precious bit of life he had.

She eased her hand from his, and he looked at her to catch the worried expression on her face.

He nodded. He would let her make the appointment.

"Does it matter what day?"

"No. I guess the sooner the better."

"Good," she said. "Thank you for letting me help."

For the first time in months, Aidan felt the slightest weight lift from his shoulders, and he wondered for a moment if what he might have been feeling was hope.

THE SOUNDS of the festival carried across the lake, tormenting Aidan almost as much as his caffeine withdrawal. He paced around the cabin half-crazed, unable to write, unable to focus, unable to think about anything but the noise and the fact that he'd give just about anything for a cup of goddamn coffee.

He needed to work. He needed to get this book done. His agent had nearly given up on nudging him about it, but Aidan felt the pressure more and more every day that passed, nonetheless. And oddly enough, since Emmy and the chaos she'd brought with her had arrived, he'd found himself able to work again. At first just a little, but he'd built up momentum every day until today—the first day he'd been unable to write a damn word.

And it was only noon. If Emmy was planning to be at the festival all day, he'd have hours to wait until she brought the coffee for him.

His nerves were shot, and he was pretty sure he'd lose his freaking mind before she came home.

He'd have to go get the coffee himself.

As soon as the thought formed in his mind, he knew he was going to do it. And he was terrified of doing it. But hell, he'd managed to leave the cabin twice in the past two days. He could get on his motorcycle and drive to town, walk into a store, buy some coffee and drive home again.

He could do that.

He was going to do it.

His stomach pitched, a cold sweat broke out on his face, and he realized he was about to throw up. He ran to the bathroom and lost his lunch in the toilet.

After another few minutes of retching, the sensation

passed and he rinsed his mouth, splashed water on his face and dried off.

Okay, so he wasn't going to be able to go anywhere if he didn't relax.

Somehow, he had to calm the hell down.

His gaze fell on the nightstand as he left the bathroom, and he saw a book that he hadn't cracked open in a while stuck under it. *Mindfulness Meditation* was the title, and someone had given it to him after he'd returned from Sudan, as a way to help him heal from the ordeal.

He'd tried the meditation techniques in the book before, and they'd certainly helped, on the rare occasions when he'd managed to sit still and do them for more than a minute or two.

No way in hell was he going to be able to sit still and meditate right now, but maybe…maybe he could at least settle his mind a little, using some meditation chants or something.

He wandered into the living room, to the front window with its majestic view of the redwoods, and he stood there staring out as he chanted, "Ohmmm… ohmmm…ohmmm…"

At first, he felt ridiculous, but after a half minute or so, he could feel himself starting to relax. He sat on the floor, crossed his legs, rested his hands on his knees, closed his eyes and continued to chant.

He forced his mind to focus on nothing but the sounds he was making, finding a rhythm between his breathing and his chanting. No more crazy-making thoughts. He pushed them away and pushed them away and pushed them away. They kept trying to return, but he guided his mind again and again to the rhythm of his breathing and the sound of his exhaled, "Ohmmmmm."

He wasn't sure how much time had passed when he opened his eyes again, but he felt calmer than he had in months. The tension had drained from his body, and his mind wasn't stuck in overdrive. He was having one thought at a time, none of them neurotic, none of them overwhelming.

It was as if he'd hit his own reset button.

Okay. So, all he had to do was drive to the store and buy some coffee. He could do that. He would simply take it one thought at a time, one step at a time, and not anticipate too far in advance.

His helmet. In the closet. He found it there, put it on. Found his boots, put them on. Found his wallet, stuck it in his back pocket. Found his keys, went to the door. Walked outside. Locked the door. Walked across the porch, down the steps, across the path to the driveway where his bike was parked.

For a moment, he had a sensation of free-falling, of being out of control, but he stopped, forced his mind back to the present moment, what he had to do next. Get on the bike, put the key in the ignition, start the engine....

The battery—what if it had died from sitting for too long?

The engine started, no problem. Nothing to worry about.

He could do this.

He gave the engine a little gas, and everything else was second nature. Before he knew it, he was on the main road, headed toward town.

Terrified and exhilarated.

He was doing this.

He had forgotten how much he loved to ride. The wind against his face, the bike rumbling beneath him—there were few things as exhilarating. This moment, right now, felt like a miracle, compared to how he'd spent the past few months.

He had gone from being a shut-in to being his old self on a motorcycle in a matter of days.

But not quite. As he neared the edge of town, the traffic increased until he was sitting at a standstill. He realized he was going to have to navigate the throngs of people crowding the streets and sidewalks for the parade that kicked off the festival. He was going to have to park at the edge of town and walk to the store.

And this thought nearly sent him back in the opposite direction toward home.

No.

He'd come this far. He wasn't going back without the damn coffee.

His body was stiff with tension again as he parked the bike on the edge of the road as close to the town center as he could get. He had to keep meditating as he went if he wanted to actually get through this without another anxiety attack.

Walking meditation…he didn't know how to do it,

but it had to be kind of self-explanatory. Just walk and focus on his breathing, in, out, in, out, one foot in front of the other until he was at the store.

He wove his way through the crowd, trying his best not to look at anyone. They were all just trees, noisy trees he needed only to navigate until he had his hands on a bag of coffee grounds. But it had been so long since he'd been to town—and even then, he hadn't spent much time there—he couldn't quite remember where the grocery store was.

There had to be a convenience store somewhere nearby. He got caught by the parade coming through and he had no choice but to stop among the onlookers as a group of clowns on stilts toddled precariously past them.

Breathe in, breathe out, he told himself. *Slowly, steadily…just breathe.*

The clowns passed, and there was a break in the slow-moving procession for him to cross the road. On the other side, he was thrilled to see the sign for People Food, the co-op that had been delivering his groceries to him. He made a beeline for the front door, and was relieved by the relative quiet once he was inside.

A woman with a pierced nose and a tattoo of a queen of hearts card on her chest stood at the counter. She looked up from the magazine she was reading and said, "Hey."

"Hi," Aidan croaked, his throat dry.

"Pretty crazy out there today."

"You're missing the parade," he said dumbly.

"I hate crowds." She smiled, and he nodded.

"I hear you."

"Can I help you with anything?"

"I need coffee."

She pointed. "Far left aisle."

Aidan followed her directions and grabbed five packages of fair-trade coffee, just to be sure he wouldn't run out soon. He made a mental note to stash some in an out-of-the-way cabinet so that he'd always have some in reserve from now on.

The clerk eyed the coffee when he set it down on the counter. "Need to stay awake for the next three months?"

He smiled…even, almost…chuckled. She smiled back at him.

"I'm Lena," she said. "You here for the weekend?"

Was this pretty little Goth chick with her dyed black hair and her barely-twenty-something body actually flirting with him?

He nearly froze up for a second, but the jolt of adrenaline from this positive, uncomplicated interaction with a pretty woman was too intoxicating not to enjoy.

"I'm actually living here, have been for months now… But I don't get out much."

Her red lips curled into an ironic little smile. "Too bad," she said, then turned her attention to ringing up his purchase.

Aidan let his gaze linger on her for a moment. Her cleavage, below the tattoo, drew his attention. She had small breasts, tantalizing the way they were pushed up and together, their upper halves revealed by a tight black tank top. She was too young for him, but her little bit of flirting had the odd effect of reminding him that he was alive. He was a living, breathing man who could actually be attractive to women, not just a nutcase who couldn't leave his own house.

He paid for his coffee, said goodbye, and left the store without the slightest bit of regret that Lena wasn't going to end up in his bed. A few years ago, it probably would have been a different story, but the past year and a half had aged him beyond recognition.

He thought of Emmy again. Emmy, with her grown-up woman's body and her just-starting-to-wrinkle hands. He sometimes felt a deep aching when he thought of her, like his soul mourning what it had lost. He thought of her, compared her to Lena—a girl he didn't know but probably could have taken home and had great sex with if he'd wanted to—and he realized how much he wanted Emmy still.

In spite of all the heartbreak.

In spite of the mistakes and betrayal.

In spite of everything.

He wanted her. Maybe it was only to wrap up their unfinished emotional business. But no. That didn't ring true in his mind. He wanted her in his bed as a lover and by his side as a companion. He wanted her in his heart where she belonged.

His thoughts kept him distracted from the crowd, but he couldn't move anywhere for a while, as several large floats were passing in front of the food co-op. Aidan was stuck watching a giant mermaid float filled with waving children, followed by a vintage truck pulling a wagon that had a rock band playing on it. The music was loud, and not very good.

But Aidan managed to hear a kid's voice beside him say, "That's my neighbor. He's a pirate."

He looked down to see Emmy's kid, Max, standing next to him, along with a little blond girl.

"Hi," Max said warily.

"Hi," Aidan answered.

His gaze immediately went searching for Emmy, and he found her a few feet away, engaged in a conversation with a tanned blond guy who looked a little too interested in Emmy for Aidan's taste.

"Mommy!" Max called to her. "Look, it's the pirate."

Emmy turned and saw them. She'd been smiling, laughing at something the dude had been saying to her. If Aidan wasn't mistaken, her body language had flirtation written all over it. She had clearly been enjoying the man's attention, and that thought turned Aidan's stomach.

His face burned hot as Emmy's expression went from smiling to shocked.

"Aidan," she said, closing the distance between them. "Wow, you're here."

He tried to speak, but his throat closed up. And he wondered if he was full-on blushing like a sixteen-year-old virgin.

He was such a goddamned idiot.

Emmy turned to the guy and said, "This is, um, my neighbor, Aidan. He's an old friend of the family staying at the main cabin on our property."

And to Aidan she said, "This is Devan. He's an old friend of my little brother's."

The dude extended his hand in greeting, but Aidan was frozen stiff now, unable to move. He grunted something that sounded like hello, and to Emmy he said, "Sorry, I have to go."

Then he turned and walked off in the opposite direction without another word. And with every step he took, he felt like a bigger and bigger fool.

Of course Emmy was with another guy. She was a beautiful, desirable woman. And she'd already made it more than clear that she didn't want him. Hell, she'd gone and married his best friend to prove it.

He'd been a fool to think he could heal the old wounds between them and make something newer and better blossom to replace the pain.

A goddamn fool.

Fury and humiliation propelled him through the crowd, across the street, onto his bike and out of town. He couldn't think of anything but getting as far away from Emmy as he could, as fast as he could, until he was back at the cabin, safely away from the crowds and noise and too-intense feelings.

His hands shaking, he set about furiously making a pot of coffee, cursing himself for being such an idiot.

Sure, he'd made it into town and bought the coffee. But was that anything to be proud of? Hell no. Any normal adult could run a freaking errand. It wasn't anything to pat himself on the back over.

The old Aidan would have responded differently to

seeing a woman he wanted flirting with another man. He'd have stuck around and made sure he was the one going home with the girl at the end of the day. He'd never had any trouble getting what he wanted that way. Now he could only run away, cowering in humiliation.

One minute, he'd been thinking of how he wanted Emmy for himself, and the next minute, he had a prime view of some other guy getting what he wanted.

Of course Emmy was the key factor there. She had no reason to want Aidan, and every reason to go for a younger, attractive guy without all the baggage.

Why go for the known quantity, already proven a failure, when there were fresh, promising possibilities to pursue?

He wasn't too crazy to know the answer to that question.

CHAPTER EIGHT

My first day on the ground in Darfur, I still
believed we could prevent a great tragedy from
happening. I had to believe we might complete
our mission there—keep the peace, save innocent
lives, prevent genocide from taking root as a way
of life—or I would not have been able to keep my
own spirits up to do the job. But by the end of that
first day, I'd seen enough death and destruction
to know that our task was a hopeless one.

From *Through a Soldier's Eyes*
by Aidan Caldwell

AFTER THE PARADE, Emmy spent much of the day in her
own booth at the festival marketplace, advertising her
business, Eco Cabin. This was her opportunity to talk
to potential customers, sell them on the ideas behind her
green prefab cabins and demonstrate her passion for her
work. And people had been enthusiastic and recep-
tive—she'd gotten over twenty leads on potential
clients.

After several hours in the booth, she closed it down
and rejoined Devan—who'd been kind enough to keep

up with Max once he'd gotten bored hanging out with Emmy—and the kids for the evening.

For such a young guy, Devan was surprisingly mature and easy to talk to. He seemed to know a little about everything, and he had a great sense of humor. She hadn't intended to spend so much time with him, but they'd bumped into each other early in the day— although she had the vaguest sense he'd actually been looking for her—and now it was already six in the evening and the festival was winding to a close.

Max and Zoe had played together beautifully all day, as far as she could tell. Now that they were face-painted, sticky from cotton candy and exhausted from the heat and activity, both kids were looking like they could use the dinner-bath-and-bed routine sooner rather than later.

Emmy considered inviting Devan and Zoe back to the cottage for a quick dinner, but then she thought of Aidan, and without analyzing why, she decided against it. For whatever reason, entertaining Devan under Aidan's nose—even with the cover of the kids— seemed cruel and unfair. She'd been so busy, she hadn't had much time to ponder his appearance at the parade. And now that she did, she wasn't sure why she felt as if she'd lost something when she'd watched Aidan walk away and disappear into the crowd.

Part of her had wanted to run after him.

She should have gone after him.

How had he even gotten to town? Had he actually driven himself? Was he safe to drive?

She thought of the coffee, of how desperate he'd seemed that morning, and she wondered if he'd really broken his exile for that alone.

Max tugged at her hand, jarring her back to reality. "I'm hungry, Mommy," he whined.

Clearly on the same train of thought, Devan said, "Would you guys like to grab some pizza or something with us?"

Emmy smiled. "Sure, that would be great."

She followed Devan and the kids as they crossed Main Street and headed left toward the local pizzeria. It would probably be jammed with people, but there was outdoor seating by the lake, and as they got closer, Emmy could see that there were still a few tables available.

They found a table right next to the lake, where the kids could play until the food arrived, and once they'd placed their order, they sat watching Max teach Zoe how to skip rocks.

"So you and Max's dad…you been split up long?" Devan asked.

Emmy had never had this kind of conversation with a guy before—having to explain her divorce to someone she might be romantically interested in. But Devan had obviously been through a break-up with the mother of his child, so he would understand better than someone who hadn't.

"Two years," she said. "It's been a rough time."

"Yeah, kids sure make it harder than you can imagine before you go through it."

"How about you and Zoe's mom?"

"Three years since we split. We never got married because we both always kind of knew we weren't right together. But when she got pregnant, we both wanted to keep the baby and give it a try. We spent half the time during her pregnancy and Zoe's first two years at each other's throats, until we finally realized Zoe would probably be happier if she didn't have to grow up around two parents fighting so much."

Emmy nodded. "Do you get along better now?"

Devan smiled. "A hundred percent better. Hannah is a great mom, and I'm happy to have had a daughter with her, but we'll never be more than coparents."

"It's wonderful you can get along with her now. My ex…" Emmy paused, never quite sure what to call Steven these days. "Max's dad, I mean, he kind of bailed out."

"Where is he now?"

"On a spiritual quest in Tibet."

"Some guys never grow up enough to be fathers."

Emmy resisted the urge to make any cynical comments of agreement. Since her divorce, she'd struggled against feelings of bitterness, and she'd reminded herself that she was at least as much to blame for the failure of her marriage as Steven was. It took two people to have a relationship, and it took two people to screw it up.

But her ex's behavior made it difficult sometimes not to rail against him. Like how he'd promised to call Max as much as possible, then hadn't, leaving their son to wonder why his daddy didn't keep his promise.

"Max misses his dad a lot, but he seems to be doing okay here. The move has given him a lot of new things to be distracted by, for now."

"Hey, I know it's not the same, but I'd be happy to hang out with him occasionally and do guy stuff with him. It would do me good, since Zoe is bored to death by fishing and rock-climbing and all those other boy things."

"Thank you," Emmy said, genuinely happy at the thought of Max getting to go fishing with another guy.

But when she pictured Max fishing it was Aidan beside him, helping him cast and reel in. Aidan, who could barely leave his cabin. Aidan, who hadn't shown the slightest interest in Max since they'd arrived at Promise Lake. Who had, in fact, only behaved with hostility toward her son.

He'd never think of offering to take Max fishing or anything else, for that matter. Why would she even want him to? The answer to that question didn't warrant scrutiny because it hinted at dreams and longings she'd abandoned when she refused Aidan's proposal all those years ago. Her life was different now and she wasn't going to let thoughts of him intrude on this perfectly nice moment in the company of a perfectly nice man.

The waitress brought them their drinks, and Emmy took a sip of her cold beer. She'd had a few over the course of the day, but she figured since she'd spread the drinking throughout the afternoon, she wasn't going to get too tipsy.

While at the same time, part of her wanted to get

tipsy and see what might happen. With her inhibitions lowered she wouldn't have to worry to death how to react to any advances Devan might make.

"How are you doing though? Since the divorce, I mean. It was probably harder on you than on Max, I'll bet."

"I'm..." She didn't often stop to analyze how she was doing. "I'm doing okay."

That was true enough. She buried herself in work and in caring for Max. She distracted herself, which she believed was mostly a healthy thing. Except when, occasionally in bed at night, she realized her life looked nothing like she'd wanted it to. All her fairy-tale dreams that she'd spun for Aidan then transferred to Steven had come crashing down around her, like so much fake scenery on a movie set.

"You look like you're more than okay," he said. "You look like you're having the time of your life."

Emmy smiled. She was feeling a little fuzzy-headed now that most of her beer was gone. She really was having the time of her life, in spite of circumstances turning out differently than she'd hoped. Here she was in one of her favorite places in the world, with her healthy, happy son and this gorgeous, funny guy to talk to.

"You're right," she said. "I am."

The way he looked at her then, she got the very distinct feeling that he wanted to have sex with her, and a delicious tingling sensation shot through her. She gazed at the lake and tried to imagine them making love.

Get FREE BOOKS and a FREE GIFT when you play the...

LAS VEGAS 7

GAME

Just scratch off the gold box with a coin. Then check below to see the gifts you get!

YES! I have scratched off the gold box. Please send me my **2 FREE BOOKS** and **FREE GIFT** for which I qualify. I understand that I am under no obligation to purchase any books as explained on the back of this card.

☐ I prefer the regular-print edition
336 HDL EVN6   135 HDL EVDV

☐ I prefer the larger-print edition
339 HDL EW9Z   139 HDL EXA

FIRST NAME   LAST NAME

ADDRESS

APT.#   CITY

(H-SR-01/09)

STATE/PROV.   ZIP/POSTAL CODE

7 7 7	Worth TWO FREE BOOKS plus 2 FREE Gifts!
🍒🍒🍒	Worth TWO FREE BOOKS!
🔔🔔♣	TRY AGAIN!

www.eHarlequin.com

Offer limited to one per household and not valid to current subscribers of Harlequin® Superromance® books. All orders subject to approval.

BUSINESS REPLY MAIL
FIRST-CLASS MAIL   PERMIT NO. 717   BUFFALO, NY

POSTAGE WILL BE PAID BY ADDRESSEE

HARLEQUIN READER SERVICE
3010 WALDEN AVE
PO BOX 1867
BUFFALO NY 14240-9952

NO POSTAGE
NECESSARY
IF MAILED
IN THE
UNITED STATES

Instead, the image of herself with Aidan formed.

Silently, she cursed herself. Maybe she was self-destructive and bound for unhappiness, when her heart and mind could turn down someone easy and uncomplicated like Devan in favor of fantasies about the most mentally unstable man she knew.

"Hey," Devan said. "I've been meaning to ask you something about that family house of yours."

"Sure. What is it?"

"I heard it's haunted. You ever have anything strange happen there?"

Emmy thought of the teacup. And the buried chest, and her missing journal that had been in it.

"Yeah, actually, I have seen a few odd things, but nothing big. Just stuff moved around to places it shouldn't be."

"You mean now, or when you were a kid?"

"In the past few weeks since I've been here. I honestly never saw anything strange as a kid."

"Maybe the ghost didn't want to scare you back then?"

Emmy shrugged. "Max has noticed stuff, but he's also not afraid. Who knows? I'm a bit skeptical of the whole thing, to tell you the truth."

"You think Max is playing tricks on you?"

Emmy mulled that over. Was it possible Max had found stuff around the property and buried it in a chest where he knew it would get dug up? He was smart enough to pull something like that off, just to perpetuate his whole pirate story.

Still, the collection of stuff in the chest had been so oddly intimate. It hadn't been stuff a little boy would think of as interesting.

She set the thoughts aside to puzzle over more later.

"It's certainly possible," she said to Devan. "He can be quite the story-teller."

Their pizza arrived, and they called the kids over to eat. As Emmy watched Devan dole out pizza slices to everyone, joking with the kids as he did so, she tried again to imagine him as a bigger part of her life—a more intimate part.

Maybe even a father to Max someday...

No. Such far-flung thoughts were only a set-up for disappointment. But the intimacy part, she had a feeling that could be right at her fingertips, if she wanted it to be.

But...

Nothing.

She couldn't make herself want Devan. Maybe she wasn't ready. Or maybe she was too screwed up to want something good and healthy in her life.

Or maybe her heart only wanted someone else entirely, someone it shouldn't want.

EMMY TUCKED MAX into bed in record time. He'd been so worn out by the festival, he hadn't even wanted to have story time, which was a first, as far as Emmy could remember.

She'd been relieved to see Aidan's motorcycle in the driveway upon returning home. Before leaving town, she'd stopped at the store to buy coffee for him, unsure whether he'd done so himself. With Max sound asleep, Emmy left the cottage door open so she could hear him through the screen door if he woke, then crossed the lawn to deliver the coffee.

She had to knock three times before he finally came to the door. He looked haggard and grouchy, his eyes accented by dark circles, his long hair disheveled.

"Sorry, did I wake you?"

"No."

"I brought the coffee you asked for."

"Oh. Thanks." He looked down at it, then up at her, but made no move to take the bag from her hands.

"Is that why you came to town, to buy coffee?"

"Yeah. I couldn't wait."

Emmy smiled, hoping to lighten his mood a bit. "Hey, whatever gets you out of the house, right?"

"I guess."

"Was it okay? Driving and being in town, I mean? I was worried about you."

"I made it home without killing anyone."

"Are you upset at me?"

"Of course not," he said, his tone full of vitriol. "What would I have to be upset at you about?"

"I don't know," Emmy said, searching her gut for the best way to handle the situation. "You seemed disturbed to see me with Devan. Maybe you were hoping that you and I would eventually...I don't know, get back together?"

"I'm not stupid, Emmy," he said.

He spoke her name as if it were a curse.

"I'm not suggesting that you are. I mean, it's just natural that, since you and I share a past, and our feelings for each other were so…intense… It's natural there might be some residual feelings for both of us, isn't it?"

"Not for you. You're ready to move on and get a fresh start and maybe nail a younger guy while you're at it, huh? Wouldn't that be the perfect post-divorce celebration?"

She flinched as if he'd slapped her. "Devan is just a friend," she said. "And you're being an asshole to suggest anything at all about my personal life. You don't know me anymore."

"Don't I?"

"No."

She wanted to throw the bag of coffee at his feet and storm away, but if marriage had taught her anything, it was that storming off didn't accomplish anything but a prolonged argument. She would stand here until this issue with Aidan was resolved.

"Let me tell you how well I know you. You dress in a hot little red bikini and frolic around here like you don't have a care in the world, which tells me you're a woman who feels confident, sexual, free…ready for action. You want male attention right now, or you'd have never put on that bikini, or that dress you're wearing today, for that matter."

Emmy felt her face burning. She was wearing her favorite summer dress, a white cotton prairie dress that made her feel young and pretty and carefree. And Aidan had just splashed mud all over it. She hated that he'd read her so easily, understanding her every desire right down to a red bikini.

Her only recourse was to deny, deny, deny.

"Sounds like you're projecting the life you want to have onto me," she said.

"I definitely don't want to prance around the lake in a glorified doily."

She hated him. She hated his guts. She'd been so proud of that bikini and of how good she looked in it, and he'd managed to piss all over that simple happiness.

"No, that's right. You just want to sit in your cabin all alone and go crazy. Of course. I forgot. You're a freaking lunatic."

And with that, she couldn't control her temper anymore. She really did throw the coffee on the ground—as hard as she could. The bag burst open, and coffee beans scattered everywhere, making little skittering noises across the wood steps.

She stormed toward the cottage, when she heard Aidan say, "I'm sorry. Please stop."

He was going to have to try harder than that.

"Emmy, wait!" She could hear his footsteps behind her, then she felt his hand grasp her arm.

She stopped but didn't turn to him.

"I'm being a jealous asshole. You're right. I'm jealous, and I wish I could be as happy as you are."

She thought of the events that had led him to this miserable place, and she instantly forgave him. She'd never risked her life in a foreign land to save anyone. She'd never been captured, held prisoner, tortured and escaped. She'd never watched friends or strangers die bloody deaths.

Her own little dramas seemed so minor in comparison. She couldn't hold it against him that she was happy and he was not.

Emmy turned and regarded at him carefully. "Thank you for the apology," she said. "Since we're going to have to live in such close proximity for a while, maybe we should try to be friends."

She knew she was blatantly ignoring the elephant under the rug—their feelings for each other—but she wasn't ready to face that yet.

"Yeah," he said. "That's probably a good idea, except I don't really want to be friends with you."

"What?"

Why did he have to make this so difficult?

"Maybe a therapist would say I'm trying to hide from my trauma by looking for a romantic relationship," he said sarcastically. "But that's not what I'm doing."

"Then what are you doing?"

"I'm remembering how I felt about you in college, and I'm discovering that I still have some of those same feelings. And I'm thinking we both might be mature enough this time around to get things right. So I want to spend time with you and see what happens."

"Those feelings...have to be laid to rest."

What she didn't say was why. She didn't explain

how she felt like an emotional refugee since her divorce, how the only relationships she could even begin to contemplate having right now were simple, easy ones. And there wasn't anything simple or easy about the love she'd shared with Aidan.

She didn't tell him that surviving a divorce had turned her into a coward, or that taking care of her son alone and keeping their lives on track took so much energy, she wasn't sure she really had any to spare for anyone else.

And she didn't tell him how she equated her feelings for him with her immature, selfish, bratty former self, the one she'd left behind, and how, now that Max's dad had flaked out on him, she had to be twice the mature, solid, rock of a parent she had been so far. She couldn't afford to go anywhere near the dumb girl who'd loved Aidan so passionately.

But maybe she should have.

His eyes, which had looked warm a second ago, went utterly dead and cold. "Right," he said in a tight voice.

Then he turned and walked away.

Emmy watched his back as he went. She didn't stop him, and she knew it was for the best. Still, she wanted to throw up, it hurt so badly watching him leave her. Why was the right thing so often the hardest thing to do?

CHAPTER NINE

I'd never killed a man before the night of our escape. As a soldier, I'd practiced, trained, prepared. But the ugly act, I'd never had the misfortune of performing, and I was glad of it. I'd hoped to go my whole life without enacting such violence on another human being.

From *Through a Soldier's Eyes*
by Aidan Caldwell

FOR THE FIRST TIME in what seemed like forever, Emmy had a night alone without Max. She should have been enjoying the freedom, but she felt restless. Max had a new best friend at day camp, a boy named Jordan, and they were having a sleepover together. Emmy had looked forward to the evening, imagining herself reading a book or watching a movie, or maybe going for a jog around the lake.

Instead, she was flitting around restlessly, doing stupid chores—paying bills, cleaning the bathroom—unable to focus on anything fun. She'd turned up the portable stereo to listen to while she worked, singing along to Joni Mitchell and whatever else the local hippie station chose to play, and the noise of it almost drowned out her thoughts.

In the couple of weeks following the Promise Festival, Emmy and Max's life at the lake had settled into a comfortable rhythm—albeit a hectic one for Emmy.

The foundation of the house was nearly complete, and soon they'd be ready to erect the cabin itself. She'd enrolled Max in summer camp, which gave her time to focus on work during the day, and he was loving the chance to play with other kids every day.

She was doing her best to avoid Aidan at all costs, because she didn't see anything positive that could come from further interaction with him after the way he'd behaved the day of the festival.

Devan had called her, but she'd made excuses for being too busy to get together, and he seemed to have gotten the message that she wasn't interested in his pursuit.

And she was furious at herself for not being interested. Why was it when a healthy, fun, romantic opportunity came along, she couldn't enjoy it? Instead, she was choosing to be alone. Maybe that was the healthiest choice she could make for herself right now... Except that her body hated the idea.

It reminded her every day that she was a red-blooded woman with physical needs and desires. And, well, her heart seemed to be protesting the matter, too, because every time she glanced at Aidan's cabin, she was struck by an almost overwhelming feeling of loneliness and desire.

As she was in the middle of rinsing the tub with the removable shower head, the lights went out and the music stopped. Emmy turned off the water and went into the other room. Lights off there, too. No sound coming from the refrigerator. No clock on the microwave oven.

Must be a power outage. But when she went to the door and looked at the cabin, she saw the lights glowing inside it against the quickly darkening night.

So Aidan had power, and she didn't. How could that be?

For a moment she thought of the chest, of the moving teacup, of her great-aunt Leticia's ghost, and she rolled her eyes at herself.

She wasn't about to get spooked by one of Max's stories, but she did glance at the chest, and she got a sick feeling in her stomach over its contents. She didn't want to look at the journal. And she didn't want to look at her great-aunt's letters, either. Both contained sentiments that belonged to other people and weren't meant for her jaded eyes. Even though she'd written some of the journal entries, she wasn't that foolish girl anymore. She didn't have that girl's feelings.

At least that's what she kept telling herself. So she continued to avoid the chest and pretended it wasn't there.

Emmy went outside to find the fuse box. Maybe she'd managed to blow a circuit somehow. But there was no box outside, and upon further inspection she found that there wasn't one inside either. Which meant that the one inside the main cabin controlled the electricity here in the guest cottage.

Which meant that Aidan had cut off her power. She went to the cabin and banged on the door. "Open up," she yelled at Aidan.

She was about to bang again when the door swung open. He stood looking at her without any emotion on his face. "What?" he said blankly.

"Did you just shut off the electricity to the cottage?"

"I needed quiet, it's too hot to close the windows, and you have terrible taste in music," he said as if that were a perfectly reasonable explanation.

"You are such an asshole," she spat before she could find any good manners to use.

"We can both agree on that. Are you done? Because I'm still in the middle of working."

"I don't give a damn about your stupid book, or about when you work, or how much quiet you need. This is my family's property, and you're lucky I've even let you stay here all this time. The least you could do is cooperate with me. I have just as much right as you to live here."

"I'm not interfering with you living your life, am I?"

"Turn my goddamn power back on."

Aidan blinked, seeming unfazed by anything she'd said. He started to close the door, and Emmy felt her fury boil over. She couldn't stand to be dismissed.

She had a flash of momentary mental clarity, a realization that she wasn't mad about the power at all. She was mad at Aidan for being here, for forcing her to face her past, for forcing her to consider how far she'd come, and how far she hadn't.

She put her hands against the panel and pushed hard, then inserted herself inside the cabin, ready to grab Aidan's computer and hurl it out the window to see how well he liked having his work ruined.

"If you're going to come in my bedroom, I'm not responsible for what happens next," he said quietly.

"What? Are you threatening me, you cowardly son of a bitch?" She was so furious, the angry words poured out.

"No, I'm just saying. Every time you've ever gotten this spitting mad at me, we've ended up in bed."

Emmy felt herself flush. She thought of their relationship all those years ago, and how they used to manufacture fights so they could have the make-up sex afterward. It had always been spectacular.

Was that what he was doing now? Did he know Max was gone for the night?

Was this just another way they'd never changed?

"I'm not young and stupid anymore," she said. "I wouldn't sleep with you if you were the last man on earth."

"Oh?"

For the first time, a slow smile spread across his lips, and it made Emmy even madder. How dare he make light of the fact that she was angry?

She wanted to hit him over the head with a lamp, or throw a shoe at him, or, or... Or strip all his clothes off and make crazy-mad love to him until they were both drenched in sweat and satiated.

She wanted Aidan.

She desperately wanted him.

Right now.

The realization struck her like thunder. She was furious that he still had the same effect on her that he'd always had. She couldn't help but want him.

And he could read her thoughts on her face, the way he'd always been able to, a quality that had given him an edge over other guys.

He closed the distance between them, his expression serious again. He looked determined, like nothing was going to distract him from the task at hand. And it was true, she didn't stop him as he took the waist of her shirt in his hands and pulled it over her head.

She stood before him wearing her white lace bra. He put his hands on her rib cage, then slowly and deliberately slid his hands to reach behind her, and undo her bra. It fell to the ground. He took his time admiring her breasts, as her nipples hardened under his scrutiny.

He exhaled a ragged breath as he slid his hands back around her rib cage and took her breasts in his palms. She ached to feel those hands all over her, demanding and pleasing as they went.

Then he pulled her close and kissed her, and it wasn't a gentle kind of do-you-want-this-too kiss. It was a firm, assertive, this-is-what-we're-going-to-do kiss, and Emmy was sure she'd never wanted a kiss so badly in her life.

She slid her arms around his neck and pulled him hard toward her as she backed up. Her legs hit the side of the bed and they fell together onto it. He was on top of her, and she could feel his erection through her pants and his. He pressed his hips between her thighs, and she spread her legs for him, so that the only thing that kept him from penetrating her was their clothing.

He pulled back for a moment, and she saw his expression, darkened with desire, still fiercely determined as he began working the button and zipper on her jeans. She helped him by pushing them down her hips. Her panties went with them, and a moment later, she lay completely naked before him.

They'd seen each other unclothed countless times during college, but this... This was an entirely different kind of unveiling. They were no longer kids, no longer in love and no longer innocent. A lifetime of heartbreak, trauma and regret stood between them now.

And Emmy's body, it wasn't the same either. It had been stretched and reshaped by pregnancy and childbirth. She liked herself better now, the way her hips were a little wider and her breasts heavier, but she had stretch marks where once there had been only smooth unblemished skin, and she had a jagged little purple scar across her lower belly where Max, unable to come out the usual way, had had to be cut out by a doctor.

She wondered how she looked in Aidan's eyes. She could read nothing but that same desire and determination in his expression.

And so she sat up and unbuckled his pants. When she got to his boxer shorts, she reached inside and found his erection, curled her fingers around him. He groaned. She began to stroke his hot, hard flesh, slowly and gently, then she pulled him closer and took him into her mouth.

He moaned louder, and muttered a curse. He tangled his fingers in her hair and moved his hips in time with her mouth, as she stroked him with her lips and tongue. She hadn't forgotten how much he loved it when she flicked her tongue against the most sensitive spot on his erection, and when she did it, he grabbed her by the hair and pulled her away from him.

"No," he said. "I want this to last longer than a minute."

He pushed her back on the bed, covered her body with his, and kissed her as his erection found her opening, where she was desperately wet and aching.

"Do you still take the pill?" he asked, his voice tight.

She nodded. She always had, and he'd remembered.

"I've been tested…and I haven't had any partners in…a long time. I'm clean."

She nodded again. "Me, too," she whispered.

And without any further delay, he thrust himself into her all the way, buried himself as deep as he could, so that she arched her back at the shock and pleasure of it, letting out a soft moan.

She'd forgotten how well he fit her, how easily their bodies accommodated each other, as if made to be together.

He began thrusting into her, fast and hard, not taking his sweet time about it, but demanding her body move with his, the way his expression had suggested he would. He watched her, his gaze locked on her face, as if trying to memorize the moment.

Emmy felt as if she were being transported back in time, for he had always looked at her that way during sex. His intensity had turned her on, but she'd never realized then, inexperienced as she was, how rare that quality would be. She had never found it again, until now.

She kept her gaze level with his, savoring him, memorizing him as he did her, and their bodies melted into one flesh. She could not say where she ended and he began. His pleasure became hers, and hers his.

But then he stopped moving his hips. "Damn it. I can't last like this," he said, breathless. "It's been too long."

Then he kissed her again, his tongue seeking out hers while his still hips drove her crazy. She squirmed beneath him, hoping to coax him back into action, but he wouldn't budge.

Instead, he withdrew from her, and his kiss moved to her cheek...her neck...her ear... Goose flesh broke out on her skin as he teased her with gentle kisses.

Then, down farther to her shoulder...her arm...her breasts... She gasped at the sensation of him sucking at her nipples, one then the other. Her fingers tangled in his hair, she wanted to keep him there longer, but he moved lower again, to her belly...her hip...her thigh... He pushed her thighs apart, and she was so eager, she strained toward him.

His mouth reached the apex of her legs, where she ached most desperately, and he worked her closer and closer to climax with his tongue. Coaxing, teasing, pleasuring…she was so close, and then she was there, wave after wave of intense pleasure crashing into her, until she was crying out and spent.

Before she could recover, he was on top of her again, inside her, stretching her in such a delicious way that he created aftershocks of her orgasm. He was thrusting, harder and faster, as deep as he could go inside her, and she could only hold on, until his own climax came.

He gasped, let out a long guttural moan, thrust one final time as his entire body tensed. She could feel him spilling into her, and she realized how long it had been since she'd really felt this one with a man…not since…

Not since she'd last lain with Aidan.

The thought struck her with its significance, but she pushed it away, not wanting to give more weight to this encounter than it deserved.

Aidan kissed her one more time, then he shifted his weight so that he lay beside and against her, with one leg still between hers and one arm draped over her belly. His head rested on the pillow next to hers, and she could feel how hot his exertion had made him.

They were simply two lonely adults with physical needs. That was all. They'd allowed sexual tension to build up between them, and this was just them relieving it.

This…what they'd done, it didn't mean they were going to get romantically involved. And it didn't mean there would even be a repeat performance. It only meant that they'd let go of their self-control and indulged in a little mindless sex for old times' sake.

Emmy had to keep reminding herself of this, as she drifted off to sleep.

AIDAN WOKE near dawn, when the light was just beginning to change the sky from black to gray, and he realized that he'd slept for the first time in months without having nightmares. He felt remarkably well-rested.

Then he rolled over and spotted Emmy next to him, and memories of the night before came rushing back, and he understood why he'd had such a good night's sleep. But that only made this feeling of well-being all the more remarkable.

He'd had sex with Emmy. And they'd slept together. And he'd slept soundly for the first time since Darfur. Emmy, who'd broken his heart and whom he'd sworn he'd never let into his heart again.

It all seemed so wildly unlikely, and yet, at the same time…

Inevitable.

It was the best sex of his life.

He stared at her in the near darkness. She slept peacefully, her expression serene. She'd always been a quiet, still sleeper. And he remembered the way he'd sometimes watched her sleep when they'd been a couple.

Back then, he'd thought he'd spend his whole life watching her sleep, waking up next to her, making love to her, laughing and living with her. He'd been such a fool. He'd had no idea of the twists and turns and crashes and burns that lay ahead.

He'd been too young, too naive, too passionate…

Too much of everything.

Now all this time lay between them, even though they were only inches apart, and he doubted they could overcome any of it. He'd be crazy to hope otherwise.

And yet…

He did hope.

All the passion between them was still there. All the energy. All the intensity. Only now, it was tempered by life experience and maturity. They had that going for them now, whereas before, they hadn't.

Emmy opened her eyes and squinted at him. "Hey," she whispered, her voice scratchy from sleep. "What time is it?"

Aidan glanced at the clock across the room. "Almost five in the morning."

She yawned. "You're awake early."

"I'm not used to getting such a good night's sleep."

"I didn't mean to fall asleep," she said. "I mean, I hope you don't mind that I stayed over."

"No, it's fine."

"Max is at a friend's house."

"I know."

She gave him an odd look but said nothing.

He probably should have been ashamed of himself for manufacturing a fight with Emmy. It had worked out better than he'd hoped. He'd merely had the childish desire to engage her somehow, because he was so damn sick of living next to her without ever being able to talk to her or touch her.

He should have been mature enough to knock on her door, but he'd known instinctively that would only lead to more frustration.

She propped herself up on her elbow, her hair falling over one eye in a way that made Aidan want to make love to her all over again. He felt his body stirring at the thought of sex.

"I just want to make sure we're both on the same page about this—I mean, what happened last night."

"What page is that?"

"I... It's just, I'm not looking for a relationship, you know?"

He felt as if she'd punched him in the gut.

"Of course. Because you've already made it clear you don't want to be with me, right?"

She winced at his words. "No. Please don't turn this into something bad."

He felt anger welling inside himself. Anger, and desire, and...the stirring of those feelings for Emmy that should have long been laid to rest.

Maybe he'd never stopped loving her, and that was why sleeping next to her was so easy now, and why it infuriated him to hear that she wasn't "looking for a relationship."

Before she could go anywhere, he grasped her around the waist and pulled her to him.

"Tell me you don't want to be with me," he said.

Then he kissed her, and she didn't resist. But she didn't kiss him back.

"Aidan," she said when he broke the kiss. "I think that aside from the fact that we've already failed as a couple, we're both in emotionally precarious places right now."

"That's bullshit," he said, his gaze locked on hers, daring her to argue with him.

She shook her head slowly. "I'm sorry, but I don't have enough energy left to love you again."

"What the hell does that mean?"

But she said nothing.

Regardless of their disagreement, his body responded eagerly to their physical contact, and his erection pressed against her belly.

When he shifted his hips so that he was pressing between her legs, she sighed and closed her eyes, clearly wanting more.

"I want you," he whispered in her ear.

She said nothing, but she slid her leg over his hip, then rolled onto him so that she straddled his hips. She sat up, her breasts dangling tantalizingly near his mouth, looked at him with an expression that held both desire and grim determination, and she shifted until he was pressing against her hot, wet opening.

And then... Then he was inside, and he felt like he would burst with that very first thrust. Her inner walls, so warm and silky and tight, held him and stroked him, driving him into blissful delirium.

He grasped her hips and met her thrusts with his own

as she rode him, and he forgot everything else except their bodies, here and now.

The rest of the world could wait.

Reality could be put on hold.

If this was all she was willing to offer him now—this sweet, heavenly taste of her body—he would take what he could get.

CHAPTER TEN

After the guard's throat was slit with the make-shift knife, I felt the ugly permanence of my actions, but I could not pause to mourn. There were three other men whose lives I'd sworn to protect, men I knew by name, men whose families and wives and children were desperate with worry about them, and I could not waste a second finding them.

From *Through a Soldier's Eyes*
by Aidan Caldwell

AIDAN SAT in the front room of the cabin on the navy chintz sofa, with the psychologist sitting in a chair across from him. Dr. Lydia Cormier was an attractive woman in her forties, with green eyes peering out from behind rectangular glasses and her blond hair swept back in a knot. She wore a simple gray suit and a pair of white high-heeled sandals that he noticed only because of the way she occasionally bobbed her left foot a little.

It was their third session together, and he had the sense that they were, as therapists like to say, making progress.

Dr. Cormier wasn't the first psychologist Aidan had seen since his time as a hostage, but she was, he had to admit, probably the best.

Emmy had booked the first appointment for him the week before, and the initial session had been mostly an information dump—Aidan telling the doctor all about why he was so screwed up, while she nodded, asked a few questions and took notes.

He felt surprisingly comfortable in her presence. She was the kind of person who instinctively knew how to put others at ease, he supposed. And for that reason, he was able to talk to her, and to talk about his experience, without having an anxiety attack.

He'd agreed to work with her two to three times a week for now, which seemed like a lot to him, but she'd said it would help him overcome the agoraphobia faster if they worked at an intense pace.

She was scribbling something on her notepad, then she looked up at him and smiled encouragingly.

"You were saying you feel frustrated by your inability to interact with people in a positive way since the hostage situation, and it's gotten worse since you came here and started working on your book."

Aidan nodded.

"Is there anyone you feel you can interact with positively? A friend or family member you're particularly close to?"

How to explain about Emmy? "There's one person. She's…a romantic interest. Or, well, we were a couple during our college years, and then we broke up. But recently, we've sort of started having a relationship again."

"Sort of?"

"We spent the night together recently, so I guess it's mostly a physical relationship...though we do talk and interact with each other, because she lives in the cottage next door."

"Oh, is this Emmy, who made the first appointment for you?"

Aidan nodded.

"How would you describe your feelings toward Emmy?"

"Maddening," he said, half joking. "I mean, I'm really attracted to her, and we have a strong physical bond, I guess."

"But not an emotional bond?"

Of course there was an emotional bond. "No, that's not right. It's just complicated. She broke up with me in college when I proposed to her, and she later married my then-best-friend. They've since split up, and..."

And what? And now he wanted Emmy back? Was he really about to say that out loud?

"Would you say you have unfinished emotional business with Emmy?"

"Maybe, maybe not. I mean, she broke my heart, and I was over her. But we're different now. We're both older, more mature, have been through heavy life stuff.... In a way it's like she's a different woman than the one I used to be in love with."

"And of course, in a sense, she is, for the reasons

you've stated. Do you feel her presence in your life now is healthy?"

"I...think it is." It felt like a revelation to say it aloud. "She got me to start talking to you, and she got me to come out of the cabin for the first time, and I don't have nightmares now...since we slept together."

"It sounds like there is still an emotional bond between you. Do you think that's a correct statement?"

Aidan nodded, mulling over her words. "Definitely, on my part. I'm not so sure about her though. She tries to keep me at a distance."

"What happened after you slept together? Did anything about your relationship change?"

"She's kind of pretended it didn't happen, I guess. We haven't talked about it. She's busy with her son and her work and with building a house."

"But she's otherwise treated you normally?"

They hadn't really talked since that night. He'd been on a high since then. Nearly floating.

"I'd say she's probably trying to ignore me."

The little stop watch the doctor kept beside her beeped, and she picked it up and turned it off. "Our time is up for today," she said. "Shall we meet again on Thursday, same time?"

"Yeah, sure."

"We'll pick up then where we've left off, about your relationship with Emmy. Until then, I'd like you to keep a journal of your ventures outdoors, how you feel during and after. Try to go outside at least once each day, and stay for a longer interval on each outing."

"Okay," he said, standing to follow her to the door.

She turned and offered him a parting smile as she walked outside. For a moment he stared through the screen door at the construction site on the other side of the property, and he couldn't believe his eyes.

He'd been keeping the curtains in this room drawn because of the hammering and building noise for the past few days, but he was pretty damn sure that the last time he'd looked, there had been no house, only a finished foundation.

But now beneath the redwoods there stood a little cabin. It was covered in some kind of rusty looking metal siding, and it had the big windows and stark, angular lines of the post-modern architecture he knew Emmy loved.

It was finished? Already? How the hell could that be?

Had she trucked the thing in on a double-wide trailer?

Driven by sheer curiosity, he pushed the screen door open and went outside. It was nearly dinner time, and no one was left at the site as far as he could tell, so he crossed the property, savoring the feel of the fresh air against his skin. The evening was still warm, but there was a slight chill in the air thanks to the trees that filtered the sun at this time of day.

He took a deep breath, and when he felt himself starting to tense up a bit, he exhaled and imagined himself blowing away all the negative thoughts and feelings.

Crazy as it sounded, it worked.

The cabin managed to look hip, modern and utterly

at home in its redwood setting. He had to hand it to Emmy, she did great design work. It reminded him of the little sketches she'd done in college of the affordable green homes she'd wanted to build. And, true to her dream, here she was, doing it.

He felt a surge of pride in his chest for her.

And then, almost immediately, an odd feeling of loss. Because she didn't belong to him, and he had no reason to feel proud of her.

Back when they were together, he'd envisioned himself supporting her in her goals, seeing her work toward her successes, both personal and professional, being there to comfort her when she faced disappointments and to celebrate with her when she achieved even the smallest accomplishments.

And now he stood outside of her dreams looking in.

But if he'd learned anything these past few years, it was that life didn't deliver what he expected. It didn't deliver what he wanted, and it didn't deliver what he dreamed of. It only gave him the mysterious twists and turns of fate, which, as far as he could tell, had no conscience and no sense of fairness either.

He walked around the perimeter of the small house, admiring its simplicity, and he remembered how he'd once imagined himself a writer, holed away in his little garret, typing out word by arduous word the Great American Novel.

And only then did it strike him that at least in this one way, his dreams had sort of come true. Against all odds, he was here, he was alive and he was a writer.

Maybe he wasn't writing any great American novel, but he was writing what was in his heart, and if he could ever finish the damn book, he believed what he had to say would change, even if just a tiny bit, the way his readers saw the world.

He couldn't think of anything more a writer could hope for.

When he neared the front door of the cabin, he heard voices, and he could see that the door was ajar. His stomach balled up with anxiety.

Emmy and Max were standing just inside, and Emmy held a picnic basket and a blanket. She placed the basket on the floor, then spread out the blanket as if they were about to have a picnic.

"Hello," he forced himself to call out, because he had to ask her how she'd managed to erect the house so fast.

Emmy turned and saw him. She was smiling, and her face was a little flushed. "Oh hey, Aidan. Come in and check the place out!"

"I don't want to interrupt—"

"Don't be silly. You're welcome to join us. We're just about to have a little celebratory picnic. Our first meal in our new home."

He stepped in the front door and looked around. "It sure went up fast. How'd you do it?"

"Sips," Max said.

"What?"

"He means S-I-P-S, also known as structural insulated panels," Emmy said. "It's a form of prefab architecture that allows homes to be built quickly and affordably, and provides some advantages over stick-built houses."

"Interesting. Like what?"

"The finished building is more airtight, for one thing, which is important here under the redwoods where it gets so damp and cold in winter. They're easier to heat and cool."

"And quicker to build."

"Yes. There are environmental advantages, too, but I'm still working through some of that, trying to find low-formaldehyde suppliers and lowest-impact materials."

Aidan watched her talking with such enthusiasm, and he saw that she was truly in her element, doing what she loved most.

"I'm really happy with how it's turned out. The construction had a few hang-ups, since this was the crew's first experience using the panels, but I sent them to training for it, and next time we work together, it will go more smoothly."

It was easy to see how happy she was. She positively glowed.

"Can I take a look around?"

"Sure, let me give you a tour," she said. "This room we're in now is the living and dining area. And in here," she said, leading him into the next room, "will be the kitchen. It's all quite small, as you can see. I'm trying to demonstrate that when space is efficiently used, we don't need much in the way of square footage."

She led him next into the three bedrooms and the bathroom. All the rooms were, as she said, small, but they were also very light, full of windows that looked out at the trees, and the overall effect was a sense of spaciousness, in spite of the fact that the place was probably no more than eight hundred square feet.

"I like how all the rooms have skylights," Aidan said. "It keeps everything nice and light."

"Yeah, I wanted to avoid the whole dark, dank feel of a lot of the houses that are built in the redwoods.

"And the skylights will help create a sort of visual balance with the solar panels that will be installed on the roof to take advantage of the hours when we do get direct sunlight."

"I'm impressed," he said as they came back into the living room.

One wall of the room was nearly all sliding glass doors that would open onto a deck, which hadn't been built yet.

"We'll have a deck here and off the master bedroom and office, as well," she said, following his line of thinking.

"What kind of floors will you put in?"

"Bamboo throughout, to keep things as sustainable as possible. This is going to be the model home for my business."

"So when someone wants you to build a house for them, they'll get a tour of yours first?"

"Yes. I intend to have about seven designs total, once I'm fully up and running. But at first I'm going to be working with three house models—this one, a two-bedroom version and a one-bedroom version."

"The others will be pretty much like this one?"

"Yes, for now. To keep things affordable, I'm trying to make it all as prefab as possible. Whatever can be produced in a factory at spec will ultimately be faster and cheaper than a custom home built on site."

He could feel the passion in her voice, and it made him want to be a part of it. He wanted to see her looking that excited about him, and not just a house.

As soon as the thought formed in his head, he realized how selfish it was, but he couldn't make the feeling go away.

So when she asked him again if he'd join them for dinner, he couldn't help saying yes.

Max had gone out into the woods to play, and Emmy called him back in to eat.

Aidan sat on the blanket and helped Emmy arrange the food, plates and utensils. She'd brought what looked like risotto with asparagus, a salad and sourdough bread, reminding Aidan of something he'd nearly forgotten about Emmy—that she was a vegetarian. He'd always loved that she couldn't eat meat because of a pet rabbit she'd had as a kid that her father had incessantly made jokes about cooking for dinner, even though it drove him a little nuts that she could be counted on never to cook a steak for dinner.

She produced a bottle of sparkling cider, and poured a cup for each of them.

Max finally came inside, out of breath, with his clothes full of pine needles.

"Go back out and dust yourself off, you little forest creature," Emmy said to him, and he did as he was told.

When they were finally all sitting together, she lifted her cup. "A toast, to new beginnings," she said.

"Cheers to that," Aidan said.

"Cheers," Max added awkwardly, following his example.

Emmy's gaze lingered on Aidan a little longer than necessary, and for the first time since she'd come back into his life, he got the tiniest sense that she desired him, not just as a lover, but as something more. She was looking at him as though she was genuinely happy to have him there.

No, he was reading too much into it. She turned her attention to serving the risotto and the rest of the food, and Aidan helped. Max produced a small rock from his pocket.

"What do you have there?" Aidan asked the kid.

"It's onyx, I think." But as soon as his plate was full of food, he lost interest in the rock and set about shoveling food into his mouth as fast as he could eat it.

"Slow down a little," his mother warned him.

Aidan tried the risotto and found it delicious. It was the first time he'd had a good home-cooked meal in months. He didn't bother to cook anything fancy for himself, and he hadn't exactly had a busy social calendar lately either.

Sitting on the blanket in Emmy's new home eating dinner, Aidan was struck by a feeling of… What? Belonging? He didn't. But he couldn't help imagining how things might have been if this were his family, and if Emmy were his woman.

Was this what having a family felt like? This sense of comfortable intimacy?

"Dare I ask how your book is going?" Emmy said, breaking the silence.

Aidan smiled a weak smile. "It's okay, you can ask. It's not going too badly, to tell the truth. The therapy sessions have helped. Thank you for pushing me toward seeing Dr. Cormier."

"Mom, I'm done, can I go back out and play now?"

They looked down at the kid's plate, and it was indeed empty.

Emmy shook her head in exasperation. "What about dessert?"

"I'll eat it later. There's an owl outside in the trees. I want to go see if it's still there."

Aidan had the sudden urge to follow Max and help him look for owls. He hadn't ever tried to interact with the kid, and part of him felt ashamed of that. He was beginning to see now though that it was mostly his anxiety and depression that had kept him wanting to stay isolated from everyone, including Max.

"Okay, don't wander too far."

She watched the kid leave, then said to Aidan, "God, I sound like such a mom now, don't I?"

"It suits you well."

She shrugged. "I do love being a mother. It's harder than I thought it would be, but it's also better than I imagined, too."

"He seems to be happy here," Aidan said. "I think you made a good move for him."

Emmy smiled. "Yeah, I knew he'd love getting away from the city. He's always been such a nature lover, just like his dad."

Aidan tensed at the mention of Steven, whom he mostly tried to pretend didn't exist. But he knew that wasn't really the healthiest way to deal with the issue.

"I'm sorry. You probably don't want to hear about Steven, I know."

He forced himself to ask, "Was it a difficult divorce?"

She nodded. "I don't think there's any such thing as an easy divorce, but having a child involved made it harder, because Max couldn't begin to understand what was going on. He just wanted both parents together and happy."

"I remember feeling the same when my parents split, but really, as an adult, I can see that what happened was for the best."

"Sure," Emmy said quietly.

"And look at how wonderfully I turned out," he joked, trying to lighten the mood. He never could stand to see Emmy looking sad.

Especially not today, when she had something so big to celebrate.

"So the therapy is helping, you think?"

"I've only had three sessions, but yeah, she seems like a good therapist, and I've been feeling a little more in control of my emotions and anxiety since she had me start keeping a journal."

"And you're sitting here right now. That's big."

He shrugged. "How could I not come outside to see this architectural marvel?"

She threw a piece of bread at him, which bounced off his shoulder and landed on the blanket. "Don't make fun of my little house."

"No, seriously, I'm amazed. It's a work of art, and it's great to see you living out your dreams."

"Yeah, a little late, and a little sidetracked, but here we are."

We. She'd said *we.*

As if she realized belatedly how she might have sounded, she looked at the floor and blushed.

"Anyway," she said, rushing to fill the silence. "Thank you for the compliment. I'm probably a little insecure about the cabin because my entire income will hinge on it being well-received by potential buyers."

"I think you've got the start of a successful business."

She looked at him, and he could see the vulnerability in her eyes then. He'd never have thought of her as vulnerable before. Not Emmy, who'd always gotten everything she ever wanted, far as he could tell. Spoiled by her parents, loved by teachers, adored by men and successful in her corporate career, it didn't seem all that likely to him that she'd fail now.

But her fear was understandable. Going into business for oneself had to be scary, especially with a kid depending on her.

He wished there was some way he could help her feel more secure about the venture, but he knew there wasn't, and she wouldn't want his help anyway. Instead, he helped her clean up the remains of the picnic. Then he thought of Max again, and he knew what he had to do.

"I'm going to go find that boy of yours and help him hunt for owls, if you don't mind," Aidan said.

Emmy seemed surprised, but she shrugged. "Sure, go for it."

So he left the cabin and walked quietly through the woods, paying attention to the in and out of his breathing as he went. Staying calm, imagining himself one of the creatures of the forest. Finally he spotted Max hunkered down staring up into the canopy of the trees.

"See something?" he whispered.

"Yeah," Max whispered back, pointing at a small owl perched on a branch above.

Aidan watched the bird with him, until the owl took off silently in search of prey, its wings spread wide. And he felt a little like the bird at that moment, stretching his wings, trying to find the parts of himself he'd lost somewhere along the way.

MAX THOUGHT it was weird how the neighbor pirate hardly came outside at all, but now he was hunched down next to him, acting all interested in the owl.

But sometimes grown-ups acted strange, and he figured pirates were probably even stranger than most grown-ups. He looked over at Aidan, when the owl was out of sight, and he thought of a bunch of questions he wanted to ask him now that the older man wasn't hiding in the cabin.

"How come you're outside?" he decided to ask first.

Aidan didn't even give him a mean look. He sort of smiled, which Max was pretty sure was the first time he'd seen the man look even a little bit happy.

"I wanted to see the owl," he said.

"Oh."

"How come *you're* outside?" Aidan asked back, which was kind of a dumb question, Max thought.

"Because I wanted to see the owl."

"Pretty cool house your mom built for you, huh?"

Max shrugged. "I'd rather live outside, or maybe in a tree house."

"I bet your mom will build you a tree house if you ask her. She's pretty good at that kind of stuff. I could even help, maybe."

Max thought about this for a minute. "But you don't like us. Why would you help?"

The man frowned. "Why do you think I don't like you?"

"Because you want us to leave, and you never come outside."

"Is that what your mom told you?"

Max shook his head.

The pirate was quiet for a while. He picked a stick off the ground and twirled it between his fingers.

He finally said, "I've been sad for a long time, and that made me act kind of…mean, I guess, and made me not want to leave my cabin. But it had nothing to do with you or your mom."

"Oh."

"It's kind of nice to have you guys around, to be honest. Do you know that in all the time I've been here, this is the first time I've seen an owl. I would never have seen one if you hadn't pointed it out to me."

Max found a stick of his own and used it to draw in the soft dirt at his feet. He drew a pirate ship with a sail on it.

"You really like pirate stuff, don't you?" Aidan asked him.

"I guess. I like the *Pirates of the Caribbean* movie. My mom said I was too young to watch it, but my grandpa let me see it anyway."

"Have you found any good treasure lately?"

Max nodded. "I know you're probably not really a pirate," he said. "But you kind of look like Captain Jack Sparrow."

Aidan laughed. "Yeah, me and Johnny Depp, we're practically twins."

"Huh?"

"Oh, nothing. Lame joke."

Grown-ups were so weird.

"Sometimes I like to make stuff up, is all. That's why I said you're a pirate, even though I always sort of knew you weren't one."

"Maybe you'll grow up to be a writer."

"Like you?"

"Yeah, but you'll be a much better writer than I am."

"Yeah," Max said. "I will. I'm already writing my first book, and it's really good."

Aidan looked like he wanted to smile but was trying not to.

"Hey, I was wondering," he said. "If maybe you'd like to go out on a nature walk with me some time."

Max shrugged. "Sure," he said, kind of like he didn't really care. But inside, his belly felt like it was getting really full of butterflies flapping their wings. He really, really wanted to go on a nature walk with Aidan. He could also feel his face kind of burning, like it did the time his mom caught him stealing cookies out of the cabinet.

The one thing he'd learned for sure from watching grown-ups was, when you wanted something bad, you were supposed to act like you didn't really care.

But then he ruined the whole thing by saying, "Tomorrow? Do you think we can go on a nature walk tomorrow?"

Aidan looked like he was tasting something gross for a second, and then he smiled again. "Sure, let's shoot for tomorrow, if your mom says it's okay."

Max stood and ran toward the cabin. He wanted to ask his mom before Aidan changed his mind.

"Hey, where you going?" Aidan asked, but Max didn't answer.

He knew better than to give any grown-up the chance to disappoint him.

CHAPTER ELEVEN

Only after we'd escaped the house where we'd
been held hostage did I understand how weak I'd
become physically. I had several unhealed
wounds, and a staph infection in my leg was close
to killing me just as efficiently as a bullet to the
head.

From *Through a Soldier's Eyes*
by Aidan Caldwell

EMMY HEARD a knock at the door, and she looked up
from her work wondering who it could be. Max was
busy coloring pictures for his treasure-hunting book,
and it was a Saturday, so no work on the house was happening.

When she opened the door and saw that it was Aidan,
she wasn't sure whether to be pleased or annoyed.

"Hey," she said. "Come on in."

"Oh, I was just, um, stopping by to see if Max still
wants to go on a nature walk with me."

"Yeah! Do you want to see my book first?" Max
chimed in without missing a beat.

Aidan cast another glance at Emmy before entering

the cottage. Inside, he looked around at the clutter of two people trying to live in what amounted to a hotel room, and he looked embarrassed.

"I'm sorry," he said. "This place has been way too small for you two, hasn't it?"

She shrugged. "It's fine. We'll be moving out soon anyway, so no worries."

In spite of the inconvenience and clutter, she'd gotten used to the tight quarters, though she thrilled at the thought of living in the new cabin soon—in a space she'd designed herself, no less. The thought intoxicated her. She'd spent her whole life imagining spaces in which to live, and now, after focusing on designs for other people, she'd finally see her imagination come to life for herself.

And in a matter of weeks, as soon as the interior work was done.

Aidan stood behind Max's chair, bent over examining the treasure-hunting book. "Great work," he said. "You're quite the illustrator."

"This is where the treasure chest was found, only, I had to draw a house there since our new cabin will be over the burial site," Max explained.

This was the first time Aidan had actually entered the cottage since they'd moved in. She observed how he filled up the space, his powerful energy drawing her eyes to him.

Since the night they'd spent together, she'd been feeling as if her body still hummed with Aidan's energy. She could hardly sleep at night because of it. Ironically, the stronger the pull she felt toward him, the more she resisted it. She knew it would be far too easy for them both to get lost in the intensity of a relationship now, when the last thing either of them needed was more emotional upheaval.

For all the reasons she listed to herself countless times, she couldn't let herself get involved with him. As much as she might desire him, she did not have the emotional reserves to help him heal and still give her son, her business and herself the attention they deserved.

"Impressive work, little man," he said to Max, and for the first time Emmy heard affection in his voice.

She imagined it was difficult for him to accept that Max was her son with Steven, and that was surely why he'd been distant toward the boy. But the way he was looking at Max now, she had a sense that maybe he'd overcome his reservations.

"What's this?" he said, looking on the bookshelf at the small-scale models of the cabins she'd designed.

"Those are models I use to show people what the finished cabins will look like. I take them to trade shows and festivals. I had a booth set up at the Promise Festival, too."

"So these are the different kinds of siding?" he asked, picking up a sample board that showed exterior finishes.

"Yes. They're all chosen to complement the natural landscapes they might be placed in."

"Since your designs are prefab, are you going to sell them on the Internet, too?"

"I've got a Web site set up, but I haven't had any orders from it yet."

Max was listening to their exchange. When there was a pause in the conversation, he said, "Are you going to live in Grandpa's cabin forever?"

Emmy watched the way Max was looking at Aidan, all wide-eyed and dreamy, and she felt sick to her stomach. He was getting attached to Aidan, even though they had barely interacted.

"No, just until I finish my book."

"When are you going to finish it?" Max asked.

"I'm not sure. Maybe by the end of the summer."

"When is that?"

Aidan shrugged. "Another month or two? It's hard to know when a book is done, and this is the first one I've ever written."

"We're writing our first books at the same time," Max said, thrilled at the idea.

"Looks like you're a much more efficient writer than I am," Aidan said.

"Can we go now?" Max said, dropping the subject.

"Sure, we'd better get out there on our walk before the day heats up too much."

"Thank you for taking him," Emmy said, as they headed for the door.

She watched them leave, and she felt old pangs of desire for Aidan mingled with fear, and dread and something new—pangs for Max to know a man in his life who would be steady and true, a man who'd always be there when he needed him.

That man was not Aidan, she knew, but some little part of her wished it could be, wished she could erase their history and make them over all anew.

"DON'T YOU EVER want to go swimming?" Max asked Aidan.

They'd been walking around the edge of the lake for a really long time, and Max felt hot and tired from the sun beating down on them. He wanted more than anything to jump in the water and cool off.

"I don't have any trunks with me. Why don't you jump in?"

Max didn't need to be told twice. He wore his swim trunks all the time now, so all he had to do was pull off his shoes and socks and T-shirt, and he was ready to swim. He undressed and took a running leap into the water. It felt so good, he couldn't help but squeal when the cold water covered his body.

Down below, his feet squished in the mud at the bottom of the lake. It felt gross, but kind of neat, too. Sometimes in the lake he was sure he could feel a fish brushing past his legs.

He looked back at the beach, where Aidan was sitting now. He was smiling, as if he liked watching Max play or something.

It made Max think of his dad and how he looked at him, which Max didn't like to think about too much. He flung himself forward in the water and practiced his doggie paddle, first toward the middle of the lake, then toward the shore until his knees were brushing the bottom. Out of breath, he stood and walked across the beach to where Aidan sat.

"You're a good swimmer," the man said.

"Yeah, I practice every day. My dad taught me how."

"Do you miss your dad?"

Max thought this was a dumb question, so he didn't say anything.

"Sorry. If you don't want to talk about it, that's cool."

Max sat on the ground throwing rocks into the water for a few minutes. Then he said, "My dad's in Tibet."

"Wow. Do you know where that is?"

Max nodded. "I have a map, and I look on Google Earth, too."

"You must be pretty tech-savvy."

"Huh?"

"I mean, you must be good at using the computer."

"Yeah, when my mom lets me anyway. She says the computer is bad for my brain."

Aidan laughed, and Max looked at him out of the corner of his eye. He liked sitting here talking to him. He wished they could do it more.

"Hey, I know sometimes it's nice to have a guy around to do things with, so, you know, whenever you want to go on a nature walk, or your mom's too busy to take you swimming, or whatever, you can come knock on my door."

"I thought you had to finish your book."

Aidan nodded. "I do, but I become a pretty dull person when I don't take a break and get outside sometimes."

"My book's almost finished," Max said. "You can read the whole thing when it's done."

"I'd really like that," Aidan said, and he sounded like he meant it.

Max looked in the man's eyes to see if he was kidding him the way grown-ups liked to do. But he looked serious.

And this made Max feel happy, the same way jumping in the lake made him happy, with no sad feelings mixed in to mess things up.

CHAPTER TWELVE

Soldiers were never meant to be peacekeepers. We train for war. We are trained to disrupt the peace, not keep it, and while I found myself often conflicted by my purpose as a soldier, I couldn't deny reality. As I rolled through Darfur on any given day amid increasing chaos, the impossibility of our situation became more and more clear.

From *Through a Soldier's Eyes*
by Aidan Caldwell

EMMY WOKE in the middle of the night with her heart pounding. She blinked into the darkness and tried to orient herself. Her face was damp with sweat, and the room seemed eerily quiet except for the low hum of the fan on the dresser.

She couldn't hear Max's noisy breathing. Only after she jumped up from her bed to check for him on the sofa did she remember that he'd gone for another sleepover at Jordan's house.

She sighed and sank onto the edge of the empty sofa as she stared out the window into the moonlit yard.

Her dream, the reason she'd woken, came back to her. Or, rather, her nightmare, in which she'd been forced to move back to San Francisco a failure, bankrupt and penniless. The worst part of it had been that she'd lost Max. He'd gone to Tibet to live with his father, because she could no longer afford to support him.

No need to look very deep to figure out the meaning of that one. Financial stress had been plaguing her constantly lately.

That, and the general fear of failing. She hadn't counted on how terrifying it would be to strike out on her own, with her own business, and the closer her bank account got to a zero balance, the tenser she became.

She wasn't even sure if she was going to be able to swing the tuition at Max's school in the fall at this rate. If she didn't get a few more clients soon, she was going to have to consider some kind of day job to keep her solvent until her business solidly took off.

If her business ever took off.

She hadn't allowed herself to consider the possibility of failure before. Which had been naive.

Aidan's presence right next door amplified that fear for her. His words upon their breakup had rung a little too true for her years ago, and she'd never forgotten them. Having him back in her life at this vulnerable time served as a constant reminder of his painfully accurate assessment of her character.

Spoiled little princess. Impulsive, foolish brat.

Maybe he hadn't slung the accusations in that order,

or even used those exact words, but his meaning had been all too clear. He didn't believe she could stand on her own two feet, and maybe he'd been right.

Emmy went to the sink and got a glass of water, then gulped it. She didn't have bad dreams often, and thanks to this one, she felt wide awake. The night was a bit warm, more humid than usual, and the house had never fully cooled off.

She was sweating, partly from her nightmare and partly from the warm air in the cottage, so she tugged off her tank top and stood in front of the fan in nothing but her boxer shorts, trying to cool off.

Her shoulders were stiff, her entire body tense, and as she became aware of the tension, she also began to realize how little she'd been taking care of herself since she moved to Promise. She had let her yoga practice slide, stopped seeing her therapist, stopped exercising regularly, stopped thinking about caring for herself at all, really. Other than her awareness of the need for a sex life, which she wasn't so sure qualified as caring for herself at all, given the sort of emotional entanglement sex inevitably brought with it.

She had tried her best to put the night with Aidan out of her mind, but it lurked in a dark corner, always half-present, reminding her that she still, against all odds, wanted him, at least physically.

And now here she was alone again, thinking about Aidan.

It only went to show how incapable she was of choosing healthy relationships.

And wasn't this relocation supposed to be about fresh starts, about taking care of Max and herself, giving them a happy, healthy life together?

If that was her goal, then she had to stop stressing out about her financial situation and start taking steps every day to make sure their lives were happy and healthy. She'd done okay for Max, but she hadn't done well for herself.

She made a mental vow to change that immediately.

She longed to be outside, away from the stifling air in the cottage, and then she thought of taking a walk to the lake now. That was a healthy, self-caring thing to do, so she would do it.

She dressed in a pair of jeans and a tank top, put on her running shoes and pulled her hair back in a ponytail. Then she stepped out into the night and took a deep breath of fresh air scented by pine needles and damp earth.

Immediately, she felt a little better. She did a few stretches to get the tension out of her body, then spotted the glow of a computer monitor on in Aidan's bedroom.

He was awake and writing at this time of night?

She had the sudden urge to tap on his door and say hello. That they were both in this quiet place in the redwoods, awake in the middle of the night, seemed like a bond they shared. Which was ridiculous.

On second thought, she knew exactly why she wanted to knock. Her desires were terribly predictable that way.

Instead, she took off down the path toward the lake,

but she hadn't made it five feet before her foot made
contact with something hard and solid, and she went
falling forward, landing painfully on her hands and
knees. She muttered a string of curses as she picked
herself up.

Further inspection revealed a large rock Max had
rolled all the way from the lakeshore to the cottage. But
he'd apparently run out of steam here in the middle of
the path and had failed to place the rock someplace safe
and out of the way.

No serious harm done, she dusted off her hands and
knees and set the rock aside, then headed for the lake.

Her walk was like a meditation, the quiet of the
woods lulling her into a much-needed sense of peacefulness. Once she reached the water, she sat beside it
to listen to its quiet lapping against the shore.

She didn't hear anyone approaching her from behind,
so when a voice said, "Hey," she started and gave a
yelp.

Emmy turned to find Aidan standing behind her. He
took a seat next to her on the sand.

"Nice night, huh?"

"Yeah. I woke up hot and stuffy, so I thought I'd get
some fresh air."

"I heard you taking a nose dive on the path."

"Oh."

Damned open windows kept her from being able to
sneeze without Aidan knowing about it.

She was painfully aware of his physical closeness
now, and she suspected he knew exactly what he was

doing in following her out here and sitting next to her—
only inches away.

She'd already demonstrated how incapable she still
was of resisting him when he was this close.

"Max is gone for the night?"

"To his friend's house again."

"Hmm," he said, and it was the most loaded non-
word she'd ever heard spoken.

If she had even an ounce of self-protective instincts,
she'd have gotten up and left at that moment. Instead,
her lower abdomen—and lower still—was turning all
liquid and warm, and the sight of Aidan's muscular
arm so close was giving her the desperate need to reach
out and touch him.

She didn't. At least she could control herself that
much.

"I like that kid, you know?"

"You're both writers."

Aidan laughed. "It must be amazing, having a kid
of your own."

"It is," she said quietly, but she had a feeling the conversation wasn't really about Max.

It was about Aidan trying to extend himself, trying
to say he wanted to be a part of her life.

She willed herself to get up and walk away before
things got any more complicated. But when she started
to move, he reached out and placed a hand on the small
of her back.

"Stay for a minute," he said. "I just want to sit here
with you."

That mere touch undid the last of her defenses. Instead of standing up, she moved closer, against him, onto his lap. She straddled his legs and grasped his shoulders and kissed him with all the hunger that had been building inside her for years.

Aidan didn't need any encouragement. In a matter of seconds they were undressing, rolling on the sand together, their limbs and desires all tangled up until it was impossible to tell which belonged to whom.

But the sand was getting everywhere, and the rocks and pebbles mixed into it poked at them. Aidan stopped and made a mat for them with their clothes, then he pulled her onto it and turned her around.

He kissed her neck, pressing himself against her backside, massaging her breasts, and the cool night air did little to cool their desire.

Then he bent her over, and when she thought she couldn't take another second of waiting, he entered her from behind, not bothering to be gentle. It didn't matter because she was already slick with desire. He was just as crazy with need as she was—a need as intense as any she'd ever felt...like starvation, or thirst, or loneliness.

He thrust into her hard and fast, and Emmy could only arch her back and urge him deeper, taking him in as far as she could. She could not get enough. No matter how hard or deep he thrust, she wanted more. More, and more, until she felt him swelling within her, then he cried out, gasping, and gave his final thrusts. His orgasm nearly put her over the edge, but not quite.

When he caught his breath, he leaned forward, and

as he kissed her back, he slid his fingers between her legs. He was still inside her, and the delicate coaxing of his fingertips was the last bit of stimulation she needed, and she fell spiraling into the pleasure that overcame her.

When her climax had passed, Aidan sat and settled her onto his lap, where he held her quietly, his face pressed against her back.

Emmy felt a mixture of joy and shame. She wanted to escape, and she wanted to stay here all night making love.

As if he could read her mind, Aidan said, "Just give me this, okay? It doesn't have to be anything more. Just this, tonight."

And she knew she would.

They eventually got cold, gathered up their clothes and walked naked back to the cottage, where they fell into bed together and made love a second time, more leisurely and tenderly than the first.

Afterward, they lay awake together, in spite of the fact that it was going to be morning soon. Emmy should have been tired, but she found herself alert and wanting to talk instead.

There was so much she didn't know about Aidan's life since they'd broken up.

She had been afraid to ask about Darfur. She wanted to ask though. She didn't feel like she could really know Aidan—this older, darker version of him—until she knew about his time in Sudan.

She lay on her side and spread her hand across his

belly, marveling at how after only a short time in the outdoors again since his confinement, his skin was already darker than hers.

He lay on his back with an arm behind his head, his eyes closed. He looked about as peaceful as she'd seen him, and it seemed wrong to ask now and upset that oasis of peace he'd found. So she stayed silent and trailed her fingertips back and forth across his belly.

"What's up?" he asked, as if reading her mood.

He'd always had an uncanny ability to read her.

"Nothing," she lied.

He opened his eyes and gave her a skeptical look. "I can feel you hovering there. You're wanting to talk about something."

She grinned. "Sorry. It's nothing."

"Go ahead," he said. "Spill."

"How's your book coming along?" she asked, which seemed as safe an introduction to the subject as she could come up with on the spot.

"Still going well since I've been seeing the therapist. I mean, I feel like my head's a little clearer now, so I can focus on it and edit it down into a cohesive story. The first draft was me sort of vomiting out everything that was in my head, with no real sense of organization about it."

"I'd like to read it. When you're done, I mean."

She watched his expression tense. "The dumbest thing about my deciding to write a book? It never occurred to me that people I know—my family and friends—would read it."

Emmy laughed. "That's how I felt about my brief stint on television."

"You were on television?"

She nodded. "I was the host of *Famous Homes of California.* I quit after shooting one season though, because the schedule was too hectic for Max."

"What was so bad about people you know seeing it?"

"The camera really does add ten pounds," she joked, then realized how stupid and shallow she sounded when compared to why Aidan probably didn't want his friends and family reading the memoir of his capture and torture at the hands of a brutal militia.

"I'm sure you looked beautiful. You always do."

He looked at her for a moment with such naked longing, Emmy felt a jolt of fear shoot through her. She was playing with fire here. She didn't want a relationship with Aidan, and all this time they were spending together—it was going to lead to one of them getting hurt.

Probably Aidan. Again. And he clearly didn't deserve another moment of pain in his life.

She withdrew her hand from his belly. Step one, cut out the physical contact. Step two, keep things unemotional.

But...

He needed a friend. Couldn't she be that for him?

"Do you not want me to read your book?" she asked.

"No, it's fine, I guess. It's just..."

"It probably feels like your worlds colliding—two worlds you probably want to keep nice and separate."

"Something like that," he said, his voice thick with emotion.

"I remember feeling that way after my divorce. I had a hard time interacting with people who'd only known me as part of a couple. I lost some friendships because of that."

Aidan nodded. "Yeah... When I came back from Africa, I felt like...like a stranger to everyone who was acting like they knew me. A stranger to my own family, even."

"I remember seeing your aunt on TV during the hostage situation, pleading for your return. It was horrifying those months."

Aidan swallowed. "I didn't like that my family, who hadn't wanted anything to do with me the rest of the time, were suddenly all interested in me once I'd come back from Africa. It was as if they wanted to get on TV and talk about me."

She knew Aidan had never been close to his mother. He'd grown up in a trailer park in Santa Rosa, to a single mother and a father who'd disappeared, and he'd worked as hard as he could to get away from that life—even getting a scholarship to Stanford. For as long as she'd known him, he'd rarely visited his family, so it wasn't hard to imagine him estranged from them now, too. It was part of the reason he'd always been close to her own father.

"It makes sense that you decided to get away then."

"I kind of took getting away to the extreme though," he said, expelling a bitter laugh.

"You've done what you needed to do to survive."

"I guess. It feels like being a coward, though."

"What was it like, being a captive?" Emmy dared to ask, unable to contain the questions any longer.

She watched his expression go from strained to oddly blank.

"Not a lot different from how I live now."

"So," she said quietly, "it's kind of like you've kept living as a captive voluntarily?"

He nodded. "Crazy, huh?"

But she could see all the scars on his body that hadn't been there before. It was almost too painful to consider what had happened to him...what might have happened.

Without meaning to, she reached over and traced a jagged scar on his side below his rib cage.

"You were tortured," she said, and saying it aloud made her stomach turn.

This person she'd once loved and cherished—though not nearly enough—had been treated as less than human, had been abused and nearly killed.

"Most of it, I can't remember very well. I guess the brain is merciful that way, erasing some of the worst memories."

"Do you remember how you got any of these scars?"

"A few, yeah."

"Could you tell me about it?"

"You don't want to hear those stories." His level gaze, dark and wary, was telling her to back off.

He looked like a stray dog who'd been backed into a corner and wasn't afraid to fight his way out.

Emmy felt her courage to push him any further falter. "Only if you want to talk about it."

"That's why you referred me to a shrink, remember?"

"I referred you to Lydia because of the agoraphobia. I don't think having a therapist replaces being able to talk about your experiences with a friend."

"Oh, is that what we're calling you now, a friend?"

His tone was sarcastic, turning his words into a slap in the face. Emmy nearly flinched.

"I hope so," she said weakly.

"Friends with benefits, huh?"

"Aidan, that's not—"

"Things with David didn't work out, huh? Did he get too serious for you?"

"His name is Devan, and we're just friends. There's no romantic interest there."

"Sure there isn't. And you swear he's not the reason you started dressing all sexy and wearing that skimpy little bikini, huh?"

Emmy flushed, then fury replaced her embarrassment. She didn't care what had happened to Aidan—it didn't give him the right to be an impossible asshole.

They'd never addressed in the light of day what had been happening between them under the cover of darkness. And Emmy had not imagined it coming up this way, like such an insult.

She'd only been seeking a little bit of solace, and she'd thought he had, too.

"It's none of your business what I wear or why I

wear it. And I never meant for you and I to become sex buddies or anything like that."

"Which is why you keep arranging for Max to have sleepovers, huh?"

He sat up, and his posture looked combative now. Emmy, sitting up, too, crossed her arms over her chest and willed herself not to flee before they'd seen this conversation through. But it would have been so much easier to run away...

"I—I wasn't really thinking about anything except that...you're lonely, I'm lonely, we both have needs—"

"I'm just the nearest convenient available male, right?"

"You're the one who followed me out to the lake tonight."

"And you're the one who hopped on my lap and started grinding your hips against me. You're just using me for sex."

"I am not!" But, she supposed, it was kind of like that. She'd been telling herself it wasn't, but it was.

She was being shallow and selfish, as he'd always accused her of being. She was taking what she wanted without regard for his feelings.

"I'm sure Devan will be happy to accommodate you from now on. Don't bother using me for sex again."

Emmy flinched at his words as he got up from the bed and started dressing.

"Aidan, please wait. I'm not finished talking about this with you."

But he buttoned his jeans and headed for the door with his shirt in his hands.

"I owe you an apology," she called after him as she rose to follow him. "I'm sorry. Now will you talk to me about this?"

Her apology garnered no response. He simply kept walking, and Emmy stopped, watching his departing form. He was too angry now to reason with.

She felt awful, and she couldn't quite put her finger on why as she went back to the bed and sat. It wasn't just that she'd hurt Aidan, and it wasn't just that he'd accused her of using him for sex.

It was more than that.

It was as if she was losing something she'd never even known she had.

CHAPTER THIRTEEN

The people of Darfur wanted to know why their lives didn't matter. They wanted to know why the world could watch them dying and not care. I've never come up with a good answer to those questions.

From *Through a Soldier's Eyes*
by Aidan Caldwell

MAX SOMETIMES thought he could see the ghost. He didn't all the way believe in ghosts, but he sort of did. It was like how he didn't really believe Aidan was a pirate, but he sort of did believe it, too.

What he saw that morning though, while he was under the bed, almost made him start all the way believing in ghosts.

What happened was, his mom was over at the new house, and he was in the cottage by himself, looking for his favorite marble that had rolled underneath the bed. He'd had to crawl to the farthest side that was against the wall before he'd gotten his fingers around the marble again, along with a big dust bunny. He was clutching both in his hand as he inched his way back to the edge of the bed.

But when he was about to crawl out, he thought he saw something moving over by the kitchen cabinet. Maybe it was just a fly buzzing around, or one of the moths that liked to flap around the lamps at night. Or maybe it was the ghost he'd been hoping to spot. He got really still and quiet like a mouse, and he watched and waited to see what would happen.

Another movement caught his eye on the other side of the room—a see-through white curtain blowing in the breeze from the open window. Through it, he could see the teacup.

Hadn't his mom moved the teacup back to the cabinet? He thought she had, but... He couldn't remember for sure.

A beam of sunlight shone through the flapping curtain, casting a square of light on the wooden floor, and he could see little things floating in the air. Dust, Max guessed. He'd once tried to convince his mom that he could see tiny fairies flying around the room, but she'd assured him the little specks weren't fairies but rather dust that came from some mysterious place.

Where *did* the dust come from, anyway? He'd demanded to know, but his mom hadn't given him a very satisfying answer. She'd said something about fibers and dirt and stuff that floated in the air.

Maybe what grown-ups thought was dust, was really ghosts, or fairies or both.

His breath caught in his throat and his belly got that

million-butterflies-flapping feeling again, because he could almost see, in the curtains, the shape of a woman. If he squinted hard, he could imagine her there, standing next to the window in the sunlight, admiring the flowery little cup and how the light shone through it and lit up the roses in a way that looked pretty.

Maybe it could have been the ghost lady's teacup from when she was alive, he decided. Maybe this had been her house a long time ago, and she wasn't a mean ghost, but just someone sad and lonely who didn't want to leave her home behind. Max understood that—he never wanted to leave here either, he loved it so much at Promise Lake.

"Max?" his mother called from outside, making him jump a little. "Could you come out here?"

The butterfly feeling disappeared from his belly, and he could no longer imagine that the curtain was really a ghost lady. Now it was just a curtain, and the dust was just dust, and nothing felt magical at all.

He slid out from under the bed and went outside, but not before deciding that he would hide under there again sometime and watch to see if a real ghost might appear.

Outside, his mom was holding a bucket and some muddy toys and sandals he'd left in the woods that morning.

"You need to wash these things off with the hose and then set them out to dry in the sun," she said.

He wanted to tell her about how he'd just seen a ghost and now he knew why the teacup kept ending up on the windowsill, but he couldn't say it. His mom looked kind of mad lately, since she started having to work all the time and worry about the house getting built right.

He didn't want to say something else that would make her even madder. So he just said, "Yes, Mom," and took the things from her.

She went back to the building site, and Max kept looking around, curious to see if he'd spot the ghost again, but he never did.

He wondered if Aidan had ever seen it, since he'd been living here longer than them. Max went to the back door of the cabin and knocked softly, even though he'd been told not to. Maybe the rule had changed now that Aidan was being nice to him. Maybe since he'd taken Max on a nature walk, he would be happy to see him now.

He waited, but when he heard footsteps on the other side of the door, he felt a little scared and thought of running away. Before he could do so, the door swung open, and Aidan was staring down at him. He didn't look too mad, but he didn't look happy either.

Max suddenly couldn't think what to say.

"Hi, Max," Aidan said, still sounding not mad but not happy either. "What's up?"

"Is it okay for me to knock on your door now?"

Aidan didn't say anything. Then he finally said, "Sure, I guess it is. It's probably best to do it later in the day, maybe around dinner time or later, because I write in the morning and afternoon."

"Oh." Max had hoped he'd say he could knock anytime.

"But if it's important," Aidan said, "you can knock anytime."

That made Max feel like he'd just gotten a new toy. He forgot about feeling scared and blurted, "Have you ever seen the ghost here?"

"No, I haven't. Why do you ask?"

"I just saw the ghost!"

Aidan frowned at him. "What do you mean?"

"I was under the bed getting a marble, but when I was about to crawl out, I saw the ghost lady. She was behind the curtain next to the window."

"Did she see you?"

Max shook his head. "No, I stayed under the bed until she was gone."

"Are you sure she wasn't a real person?"

"No, she was a ghost. I could only see her by the shape of the curtain."

Aidan frowned again. "Have you told your mom about this?"

Max shook his head. "Don't tell her."

"Why not?"

"She'll be worried."

"I think she'd like to know, though."

"She's always worrying about things."

Aidan knelt in front of him and looked at him real serious. "It's wrong to keep things from your mom, but I need to know if this ghost you saw is kind of like how you said I was a pirate."

"You mean, am I making it up?"

Aidan nodded.

Max thought about it. He could see Aidan didn't really believe him, and if Max kept insisting the ghost was real, Aidan would tell his mom. Then she'd get even more worried about him.

"Yeah, it's like how I said you were a pirate," Max said, disappointed that he hadn't managed to convince Aidan of his story.

He still didn't know for sure if Aidan was a pirate. He might really be one...

"Okay, so you imagined the ghost?"

Max nodded, a little angry that Aidan wasn't willing to go along with the story. He'd been sure the man would understand.

"Are you the one who keeps moving the teacup?"

Max didn't say anything. He didn't want to keep lying.

"Go put it back in the cupboard where it belongs, okay?"

"But, the ghost will come move it again."

Aidan gave him a look that said Max had better stop arguing, so he didn't say anything else. He turned and stared at the ground as he walked back toward the cabin.

Grown-ups just didn't understand.

EMMY STOOD in the driveway and watched the top of her son's head in the backseat of her mother's silver Mercedes as it pulled away and disappeared down the road. An impossible sadness filled her chest, which was ridiculous, since just the day before, she'd been desperate to buy herself a little time alone.

A few days ago, the weight of single parenthood in the midst of starting a new business and building a house had been weighing heavily on her. She'd called her mother and asked her if she might include Max on her upcoming trip to Lake Tahoe, and Emmy had been grateful when her mother had happily agreed to the plan. Max, too, was excited about a week with his grand-mother, who spoiled him horribly, let him stay up late and devoted all her time to entertaining him. And this morning, he'd sat on the front steps waiting to see her car pull up.

But this was Emmy's first time saying goodbye to Max for more than an overnight in several years. And she'd been unprepared for how hard it would be. She went back inside and paced around the house under the guise of straightening things up, but mostly she was trying to keep herself busy so she wouldn't curl up on the bed and cry all day.

Pausing on her way to the kitchen to put away a plastic cup Max had left on the coffee table, she looked out the window at Aidan's motorcycle parked nearby, as it always was. Something else was bothering her besides her son's departure. Without Max around, what was keeping her away from Aidan?

Nothing at all, except for the fact that they'd barely spoken since the last time they'd slept together.

All alone now, she could do whatever she wanted, and there'd be no one but herself to answer to. She could hang out at the local bar and have a drink with other grown-ups. She could connect with old friends. She could lie around reading for hours at a time....

But she wanted Aidan. Maybe it was habit, from having gone to him the last two times Max was away. But as she let herself contemplate being with him again, Emmy could hardly stand the empty space between herself and Aidan.

And she would have to resist it. She was being selfish again, not thinking about his feelings. If she wasn't willing to have a relationship with him, she needed to stay away, which was going to be a tall task for the next week. She'd bury herself in work instead. She'd get totally caught up so that when Max returned, she'd feel refreshed and ready for life as a single mom again.

And there was one other thing she'd been wanting to attend to. Pausing in the middle of putting away her swimsuit that had been hanging to dry, she glanced warily at the chest in the corner of the room.

She needed to go through it to get rid of her sense of unrest surrounding it.

So she poured herself a glass of red wine, and she made herself sit on the floor with the chest and open it up.

There was the journal she dreaded seeing again, its red cover aged but still beautiful.

She opened it up and read Aidan's poem about the kite. Tears formed in her eyes. He had loved her more than any man ever had or ever would again, she feared. And she'd ruined it.

She read through their entries, one after another, until she felt as if she'd been kicked in the stomach repeatedly, and her face and the front of her shirt were covered in tears. She looked at the pictures, at their young happy faces smiling toward a future they had no idea would end up so fractured and wrong, and she mourned the loss of their innocence.

She saw the ticket stubs for their trip to Reggae on the River, where they'd danced and drank and swum the entire weekend all those years ago, so ridiculously happy and filthy and high on life. It had been the last happy weekend they'd ever spent together, because he'd proposed to her at the end of it, lying outside one night as they gazed up at the stars and listened to the sounds of reggae drifting through the air, and she'd said no.

She'd ruined it all.

She'd been too afraid of how much he loved her, and how little of the world she'd experienced. If she'd married Aidan, her first love, how would she know if there was anyone better for her out there? She'd wanted to be free and experience other men. Other men like Steven.

And look how that had turned out.

She hadn't deserved Aidan's undying love back then, and she didn't deserve it now.

By the end of the journal, she knew she had to leave him alone, because all this passion they'd shared was a fire that would scorch them both if they let it burn again.

She set aside the journal, and began reading the letters in the chest, in order from earliest to latest dates. They'd all been letters to Leticia Van Amsted from a man named Walter Elliot.

He'd loved her, and she'd broken his heart. He'd wanted to marry her, and she'd said no.

Just like Emmy and Aidan.

She didn't know how or why her journal had ended up with Leticia's letters, both tales of love affairs gone wrong, but she could see why they belonged together now, and when she was done reading, she placed them back in the chest and closed it tightly. She didn't intend to open it again. Then she said a silent goodbye one final time to the mementoes of two love affairs dead and gone.

CHAPTER FOURTEEN

What can we learn from a tragedy like Darfur?
When will we decide that genocide can never be
tolerated? That turning our eyes away from the
horror will not make it go away?

From *Through a Soldier's Eyes*
by Aidan Caldwell

AIDAN COULD finally see the end of his book. He'd been
revising and editing for weeks, and at last, he had the
sense that he was nearing the conclusion.

He rarely logged on to the Internet for fear of
seeing a news headline, but he did so now just long
enough to check his e-mail. A message from his
literary agent, dated three weeks ago, waited for him.
He opened it and read that his agent was checking on
the book's progress.

For once, he happily clicked reply on the message
and typed out that he expected to be couriering the
manuscript in another week.

Another week? Was that right? Was he really going
to be done that soon?

He was.

The idea stopped him cold. What would he do after the book was done? Sure, there'd be revisions and other little details to wrap up once the manuscript was turned in, but those things wouldn't consume his whole life the way writing the book had.

So what would he do?

It was a question he'd tried hard not to consider. And he didn't want to have to imagine moving on from the cabin and finding a new life in the outside world.

A new life where? Doing what? He hadn't a clue. He'd been too consumed by the book, and by his recovery, to consider such questions.

Emmy's father would surely let him stay at the cabin for as long as he wanted, but he couldn't hide out here forever.

Plus he needed to get away from Emmy.

She was settling into a new life here, and he wasn't a part of it unless he wanted to be her sex buddy. That much was crystal-clear.

Somewhere along the way, he'd gotten sucked in yet again to the fantasy of him and her together, a couple once more, and he'd let it blind him to the reality that he had a future to plan for himself.

Alone.

As he hit Send on the message to his agent, he watched the list of his unread messages reappear, and he scanned them to see if any were worth opening. When he saw the name of his closest friend from their captivity in Darfur, his breath caught in his throat.

Garrett McKinley, Captain, U.S. Army, the name on

the message read, accompanied by the subject line, "Where the hell'd you go, man?"

Aidan's mouth went dry as he opened the message.

Garrett had been there with him through everything. More than anyone else on earth, he knew.

He really knew.

Aidan read quickly. Garrett had left the army just as Aidan had, had spent his time recovering by doing the Tour D'Afrique, a bicycle race from the top to the bottom of the African continent, during which he'd raised sponsorship money to help the people of Darfur. And that had led him to start his own aid organization for the crisis in Sudan.

He wanted Aidan to join him in his work. He said he needed someone who knew the country as well as Aidan did, and he was hoping the publicity from Aidan's book would, by association, bring awareness to their cause as well.

The timing of the e-mail was eerily perfect. Aidan stared at his computer screen for only a few moments before he knew what he was going to do. He clicked Reply, then told his friend that he'd love to help, that he could be on a plane in as little as a week—as soon as his book was done. He included the phone number at the cabin and asked Garrett to call him as soon as possible.

So, he had a plan and a purpose now. He'd be leaving the cabin, and he'd be going back to Africa. He could do revisions on the book and take care of anything else his editor requested from there, no problem.

He was going back to Africa.

The thought both terrified him and felt absolutely necessary. He had to do it. He would face the ghosts that haunted him, and he would lay them to rest once and for all.

Before he could change his mind, he wanted to tell Emmy.

Okay, maybe he was hoping to torture her a little with the information. But he doubted it would have that effect anyway. Still he wanted to share the news. Mostly he wanted to make the decision more real by saying it aloud to someone.

He stood and went to the window. Emmy was nowhere in sight. Then he remembered that she was moving into the new house now, which he couldn't see from his cabin.

Aidan put on his shoes and headed for the front door, just in time to see a furniture delivery truck coming up the driveway. He went outside and walked toward the woods as several men climbed out of the truck and began unloading something from the back.

He watched as Emmy met the man at the truck. Aidan went to the deck to wait until they were finished.

He marveled at his ability to go outside, to face strangers even, without feeling afraid anymore.

He had Emmy to thank for that, and the thought made his throat tighten. He hadn't given her enough credit for the positive ways in which she'd influenced his life and his recovery. He'd been too blinded by the pain from what she wouldn't give him to see the gifts she had brought.

She looked fresh and happy today, as she talked with

the furniture deliverymen. She wore a green cotton sundress that glided over her curves beautifully and accented her smooth, angular shoulders with little spaghetti straps that tied at the top.

The men began carrying a couch toward the cabin, and Emmy came back to the deck, surprised to see him there waiting for her.

"Hi," she said. "I'm finally filling this place with some furniture."

"Congratulations."

"I got two jobs this week," she said, unable to contain the huge smile that lit up her face.

"Two?"

"An order for a three-bedroom cabin on the other side of the lake, and an order for a one-bedroom over in Leightonville."

"Word's spreading about your talent."

"I attended a green-energy festival last weekend—that's what brought me the new business."

"That's great. I'm happy for you."

"It's a huge relief. I was down to the bottom of my savings account when this money came in. Hence the furniture order," she said, grinning.

"I've got a little news of my own," he started to say, but she interrupted him.

"Oh, before I forget! My mom's coming back from vacation with Max tomorrow, and I thought you might like to join us all for dinner."

"Thanks," Aidan said. "I—I'm not sure I can make it, but I'll try."

"Sorry, what was your news?"

"I'm going to be leaving the cabin in about a week. I'm almost finished with the book, and I got an offer to join a friend working for a nonprofit in Africa."

Emmy looked shocked. "Oh, wow. So soon."

"I've been here long enough. I mean, I certainly managed to get in your way plenty."

"I've just gotten used to having you here. I guess I stopped hoping you'd leave so I could have the cabin a long time ago." She flashed a rueful grin.

"Have you thought about living in the main cabin so that you can keep the new one in model-home condition for your business?"

"That was my original plan. But...I don't know. I feel like I should live in the place so people can see what it's really like to live there—where I store my stuff, how the place looks fully lived in. It seems a more honest way to sell what I'm offering."

Aidan nodded. "Sounds like a tall order for a single mom to accomplish—keeping the kid on his toes for impromptu open houses?"

"Perhaps, but I'm going to try. It'll be good motivation to keep the house clean, anyway."

"Maybe hire a housekeeper," he said, thinking that's what the Emmy he'd known would automatically do. She'd been raised with other people doing her bidding.

"No, I don't want Max to grow up like I did. I want him to experience the collaborative work it takes to keep a household running."

Aidan blinked at her words. She really had changed. She wasn't the same spoiled princess anymore.

But she wasn't his, either. He wasn't going to torture himself anymore with wanting what he couldn't have.

He had to let go.

Leaving Promise Lake would be his final act of letting go, and it would come not a moment too soon. Part of him ached at the thought of leaving Emmy—and Max, he realized—while another part of him could not wait to get away from the dull, throbbing pain their presence in his life created.

"It won't be the same around here without you," she said.

"Max will have to find a new pirate to observe."

"He's going to be sad to see you go," she said quietly, and he could read on her face that she regretted having let him and the kid spend time together.

Now he would be yet another man walking out of Max's life. But not for good. He'd stay in touch, if Max wanted that. He'd send him things from Africa, and he'd come back to visit when he could....

Hell, who was he kidding? He wasn't Max's father, and he certainly couldn't be his deadbeat dad either.

"I'll miss that kid," he said, but one of the deliverymen stopped to ask Emmy where she wanted the desk they were about to unload.

"In the last bedroom," she said. Then to Aidan, "If you could send him a few mementoes from Africa, he'd really love it."

"Of course I will."

She looked as if she wanted to say something else, but she didn't. Instead, she reached out and touched his arm, gripped it gently in her hand for a moment then let go. He almost thought she was going to cry, but her expression remained only solemn.

"I'll…be sad to see you go, too," she finally said.

"Now don't go getting all mushy on me," Aidan joked. "I know you're lying anyway. You've got another week to put up with me."

He couldn't take any more of this, so he took a step back and turned toward the cabin.

Part of him expected Emmy to stop him, to tell him he couldn't leave because she was in love with him, but that was the same foolish part of him that had believed all along she wanted him when she didn't.

So he walked away, and she didn't stop him. He vowed it was the last time he'd ever let that happen.

EMMY TOLD HERSELF she was glad Aidan was leaving. She told herself it was a huge relief. She didn't want him in her family cabin, constantly underfoot, and when he was gone, her life at Promise Lake really would be a fresh start, free of ghosts from the past.

Max's return from his time with his grandmother was a welcome reunion. She'd had time to recharge and catch up on work, and start getting them moved into the new house, and she was thrilled to have her boy back.

But on his first day home, she made the mistake of telling him that Aidan was leaving soon.

Max felt far differently than she did about Aidan's departure.

"But why is he leaving?" Max said, kicking the back of the new sofa so that Emmy had to bite her tongue to keep from scolding him too harshly.

"I understand you're upset, but please don't kick the furniture," she said calmly.

Once in a rare while, she managed to impress herself with her parenting skills.

"He doesn't want to be around us anymore?"

"That's not it at all, sweetie." She took his hand and led him around the sofa, then sat and pulled him onto her lap. He smelled like trees and dust, and she buried her nose in his hair for a moment.

"He's finished writing his book, and he has a new job to go to far away from here," she explained.

"Is he going to Tibet, too?"

Emmy winced. Tibet, to Max, was probably the place men went to escape him. "No, he's going to a country in Africa, I think."

"Oh," he said, sounding dejected.

"I know it's hard when a friend leaves, but on the bright side, we've been making lots of new friends since we moved here, haven't we?"

"I guess. Who will live in the cabin when Aidan leaves?"

"I suppose it'll go back to sitting empty unless someone in our family wants to use it."

"Can I make a fort there?"

"Sure you can, any time you want."

He seemed momentarily satisfied with this idea. "Can we call Daddy?"

Emmy's stomach knotted. "I don't have a way to reach him by phone, remember?"

"Why did he have to go where he doesn't have a phone?"

Good question, Emmy wanted to say, but she did her best to stick to her policy of never bad-mouthing Max's dad.

"He's trying to figure out some things about his life. Sometimes grown-ups need to do that by going far away and not talking to people for a while."

"What's he trying to figure out?"

"I'm not sure. Maybe when he gets back, you can ask him what he figured out."

"When is he coming back?"

"I don't know, sweetie."

"Do you think he'll bring me a present?"

"I bet he will. He loves you very much, even when he's far away."

Max went silent, and Emmy blinked at the burning sensation in her eyes. Now was not the time to be getting teary-eyed.

She didn't want her son ever having to doubt his father's feelings. But unfortunately, Steven lived his life in such a way that inevitably everyone doubted his feelings at some point or another. On the surface he was likeable and socially adept, but beneath the shiny veneer, he was a man who put himself first. He had a hard time thinking beyond his own immediate desires to see anything else—even the needs of his son.

"I think I'm going to write another book," Max finally said.

Emmy smiled and hugged him close. He tried to squirm away. "Oh yeah? What about?" she asked.

"About ghosts."

"Really? Why ghosts?"

"Because you know how we found the treasure chest? I think a ghost put that stuff in it. And I saw a ghost in the cottage one day, too."

Emmy weighed Max's reasoning about the contents of the chest. His idea was as good as any she'd come up with. But then his second comment sunk in.

"What do you mean you saw a ghost in the cottage?"

She listened to Max's description of a woman's shape behind a sunlit curtain, and the hairs on the back of her neck stood up.

"Can you tell me exactly what the woman looked like?"

Max shrugged. "Not really. She was just a see-through shape."

"Was she young or old?"

"She was a grown-up, like you."

"But was she my age, or more like Grandma's age?"

"She was like you," he said vaguely.

Emmy sighed. This sounded more like one of Max's tall tales than an actual event. He had such an active imagination, there was no way he could hear a ghost story without it coming alive in his head.

Still, when she thought of the contents of the chest, and of the odd feeling she'd sometimes gotten at night in the cottage…

No.

She couldn't let the imagination of a little boy get her off on such a ridiculous track.

"Max, it's okay to write a story about ghosts, so long as thinking about them doesn't scare you."

"I'm not scared of ghosts. The one I saw was nice. She just wanted to look at the teacup sitting in the sunlight."

Emmy resisted the urge to insist there were no such things as ghosts. She sensed that Max needed her to believe in him right now, and what he didn't need was some grown-up crushing his ability to distract himself from the harsher realities of life.

Like people he cared about leaving.

Emmy blinked away the tears in her eyes and gave her son one more hug before he wiggled out of her arms and went about his little-boy business.

CHAPTER FIFTEEN

After being flown out of Africa, we were taken
to an air force base in Germany for medical care.
It was in those slow-moving days at a hospital in
Landstuhl that I began to process what had happened. The nightmares began, and sleep became
a luxury I didn't often enjoy.

From *Through a Soldier's Eyes*
by Aidan Caldwell

EMMY WAS in the middle of folding laundry when the
phone rang. She picked it up half-distracted.

"Hello?"

"Emmy, hi. It's Steven."

She was unprepared for the sound of her ex-
husband's voice on the other end of the line. Finally.
Like a slap in the face.

"Oh, um, hi," she forced herself to say. "Where are
you?"

"I'm still in Tibet. I was calling to talk to Max."

Of course. It was so like Steven to call out of the
blue, as if he hadn't disappeared at all, as if his promise

to call frequently then not doing so meant nothing to his son's well-being.

She wanted to scream, curse or hang up the phone. But she couldn't. None of that behavior would help Max, and it wouldn't make Steven change. She simply had to accept that Steven was careless. He always had been, always would be.

Emmy's stomach lurched when she peered outside at Max happily playing on the deck, creating some sort of maze with twigs and rocks, for bugs to navigate. Hearing from his father, even when he wanted to, was going to be emotionally trying for him.

She thought of lying and saying Max wasn't home, that Steven would have to call back later, just so she could give Max a chance to prepare mentally for the phone call. But she knew the second call might not come, so she would have to take her chances.

"Okay," she said, ending the awkward silence. "He's been looking forward to hearing from you. He's looked Tibet up on maps and Google Earth."

"That's cool."

How about asking how his son was doing, what his life was like, how he'd adjusted to being abandoned by his father?

When no questions came, she bit her tongue, put Steven on hold and went out to the deck for Max.

"Hey, sweetie, you just got a surprise phone call."

Max looked up from his maze-building distractedly. "I don't want to talk on the phone."

That was his typical response. He hated phones and hated when his grandmother insisted he talk to her.

"It's your dad," she said in the cheeriest voice she could muster. "Calling all the way from Tibet."

She could see the warring emotions in his expression—pain, loss, hope, love… He was reluctant to hear from his dad, no matter how much he wanted to, because it would mean feeling all the awful things that went along with not having his father here with him.

He kept lining up twigs for his maze.

"Max, sweetie, I want you to come in and talk on the phone to your dad. You can tell him all about what you've been doing this summer—your pirate book, the treasure chest, how good you've gotten at swimming—"

"No!" he said, then sprang off the deck and ran toward the woods.

"Max! Come back here!"

Emmy watched, bewildered, as he disappeared.

She went back to the phone. "Max isn't up for talking right now," she said.

"I'm headed to a meditation retreat in the mountains for the next week. I won't be able to call while I'm there."

"I think he's missing you a lot, but he doesn't know what to do with the feelings. He just ran off into the woods when I told him you were on the phone."

She wasn't consciously trying to give Steven a guilt trip, but after the words had left her mouth, she realized that might be how she'd sounded. Oh well, she'd only presented the facts.

But Steven was apparently far too Zen to react with

any kind of hostility. "Okay," he said mildly. "Should I try calling again next time I'm near a phone?"

"Of course you should." Emmy had trouble containing the annoyance in her voice. "Regardless of how he reacts, he needs to know you care enough to call him."

They said their goodbyes, and when Emmy had placed the phone back on its receiver, she went outside to look for Max. The woods were dark and cool at this time of day, and silent, too. She couldn't hear the sound of footsteps, and she had no idea where to look for Max.

Sometimes she had trouble remembering why she'd ever loved Steven. They'd met while she was still dating Aidan, of course, and she'd always thought of him as Aidan's tall, dark and quiet best friend. He'd had an air of aristocracy about him that came from having grown up ridiculously privileged—his background made her own relatively wealthy family look like a bunch of hicks—and he was the polar opposite of Aidan.

Where Aidan was passionate and aggressive, Steven was cool and passive. Where Aidan was wild and untamable, Steven was as tamed and manicured as a French garden. Where Aidan spoke plainly and bluntly, Steven knew how to talk around an issue until she couldn't remember what the issue had been in the first place.

It was a miracle Aidan and Steven had ever been best friends, but they'd gotten to know each other as roommates in the college dorms freshman year and had been fascinated by their stark differences. Emmy could sort of see how they balanced each other out as friends, but back then, she'd been immature enough to think that the man she didn't have might be exactly the one she wanted.

Emmy had been a fool in those days. She'd been scared of all Aidan's passion. She'd been unsure what she wanted in life, and Aidan's insistence that she was what he wanted only pushed her away.

She'd never expected, upon their breakup, that she'd really end up marrying Steven. She'd harbored a bit of a crush on him, sure, but she'd considered him off limits because he was Aidan's friend. And then...

Well, then life happened.

A party they'd both attended after Aidan had left to join the army, had resulted in a little too much drinking, which led to some flirting, which led where such things often did.

Looking back, she could see the mistakes she'd made so very clearly. Steven hadn't really been all that appealing to her for his own merits as a potential mate. Rather the appeal had been in his newness; he was a flavor of man she hadn't tried yet.

And after the passionate intensity of her years with Aidan, the ups and downs of their young relationship, she couldn't help finding someone so different appealing. Steven had seemed mature, stable and similar to her. But she mistook lack of passion for maturity, and she mistook aloofness for a sign of depth.

Steven was nothing more than a spoiled rich boy who'd never had to face any challenge in life. He always got what he wanted, whether it was a new car or a new lover. So it seemed natural to him that if he wanted to sleep with the nanny, he should do that, and if he wanted to take off on a spiritual quest without regard for his son's needs, he should do that, too.

Not that Emmy was bitter or anything.

Still not spotting any sign of Max in the nearby woods, she felt panic growing in her belly. Surely he wouldn't go off so far that he got lost—he'd never been a risk-taker—but he might have gotten disoriented if he was very upset. She backtracked, heading toward the cabin, trying to imagine where a kid would go if he wanted to hide.

Five minutes later, she was knocking on Aidan's door to ask if he'd seen any sign of Max.

He answered looking like he'd just woken up.

"Sorry to bother you," she said. "But I've lost Max. He ran off a little while ago. Any chance you've seen him?"

"No, sorry. I had a headache and went to lie down for a little while."

"Well, if you wouldn't mind keeping an eye out, I'd appreciate it."

He frowned and ran his fingers through his hair, the way he always used to when he was waking up. Emmy felt a little stirring of nostalgic affection in her chest.

"I'll help you look for him," he said. "Let me grab my shoes."

"Thanks," she said. "I appreciate it."

A minute later, he had his shoes on and they were

headed toward the lake, Aidan taking the eastern direction and Emmy the western.

She called out for Max repeatedly, but got no sign of him. And after another twenty minutes of searching, plus a return to the house to see if he was there, she was in full-on panic mode. Horrific images of what might have happened to him crowded her head, and she was on the verge of tears as she went looking for Aidan near the shore of the lake again.

When she spotted him sitting next to Max, the two of them with their heads bent over something, she breathed a huge sigh of relief, and tears of joy stung her eyes.

"Hey!" she called out. "Where have you been?"

Aidan looked up at her, and as she neared he said, "I'm sorry. I just found him here. I was about to bring him to you."

"Max," she said. "Sweetie, you can't run away like that any more, okay?"

"Sorry," he said, distracted by a delicate bird's nest that he was holding. "I found this," he said, as if that were a perfectly good explanation for disappearing.

To him, it was.

Emmy knelt next to them to look at the nest, which she could see now contained a red ribbon woven among the twigs and leaves. "It's beautiful," she said.

And it was. It reminded her of the tiny red woodpecker's feather she'd found in the woods as a child, and how absolutely in love with that feather she'd been. It had been her treasure, and this was Max's treasure.

She couldn't ruin the moment with a lecture about forest safety.

Someday Max might look back on this time as some of the most magical days of his life. Surely he would. The pristine lake, the majestic redwood trees, the peacefulness of the forest, there was no way not to find magic and wonder here.

And he would remember her and Aidan being a part of it all, she realized as she looked at the three of them here together, examining a bird's nest. This intimate little scene, it made them look like a family, when they were anything but.

They were barely friends, the three of them. She hadn't intended Aidan to be a part of her son's memories, a part of his childhood, but he was fast becoming a significant part of it all, and some wistful part of her wanted him to settle into that spot he'd come to occupy and call it home.

Call it family.

"You see how the bird used little bits of mud to make all the pieces stick together?" Aidan was saying to Max.

He nodded. "Yeah. Right there, and there."

"Wonder where that ribbon came from."

"Maybe the bird found it on the beach. It could have fallen out of someone's hair," Max said.

As an architect, Emmy couldn't help but admire the delicate balance the bird had struck to create its home. Her job was not so different, really, when she designed a house.

And a home, no matter whether it was for a bird or

a person, involved striking a complicated balance. Not just in the physical structure, but in the emotional structure, too.

What if it were only her and Max living in their nest for the rest of his childhood? Would that be the balance he needed? Would he always recoil in fear when it came to interacting with his father?

Emmy didn't have the answers, but she knew she wanted to give Max the best possible home to grow up in, one that nurtured and protected him, provided him a safe haven in which to thrive and grow both physically and emotionally.

"You could make a little house like that, you know, if you studied the bird's construction methods," Emmy said to Max.

His eyes lit up with excitement. "Yeah!" he said. "I want to do that. I'm gonna start collecting twigs now. Can you hold this for me?" he said to Aidan as he clambered to his feet.

"Sure." Aidan took the nest and smiled up at Emmy.

"Don't go any farther than the house, okay?" Emmy called after him.

"Okay, Mom!"

She watched as he stopped at the nearest tree and started gathering twigs from the ground around it.

When he was out of earshot, she said to Aidan, "Thank you for finding him. His dad called a little while ago. He got upset and ran off instead of talking to him."

"Must be rough on the kid, having his father so far away."

Emmy nodded. "It's hard with kids so young. They don't know why they feel what they do, and they don't know what to do with any of the feelings."

"It looks like you're doing a fine job with him. He'll be okay, especially since he's got a mom as great as you taking care of him."

Emmy hadn't expected the compliment, and she found herself stunned silent for a moment. Aidan actually thought she was a good mother?

Unexpected tears welled up in her eyes. She didn't go around wondering if the rest of the world thought she was a good mother. She wasn't one of those women whose greatest aspiration in life was to win the title Best Mom Ever. But, in her efforts to redefine herself since the divorce, to hold onto herself, to hold onto her personal and career dreams, she had to fight the insecurity that she wasn't doing as well as she could for Max.

Weren't mothers supposed to sacrifice everything for their kids? Or was sacrificing everything for anyone, to the point of unhappiness, any way to live in the world?

Emmy didn't think so, and she felt as if she'd been gambling Max's well-being on the assumption.

Maybe, in all the sadness and upheaval of the past few years, she really had managed to be both her own woman and a good mother.

The idea felt like a precious gift Aidan was handing to her.

Before she could thank him, he stood, examining the bird's nest. "Pretty neat treasure he found here, eh?"

That reminded her of the treasure chest they'd all opened together. She'd never talked to Aidan about it.

"Remember those letters we found in the chest?" she said.

"Sure."

"I read through them all. It was fascinating. They're love letters to my dead great-aunt."

"Yeah? Ever figure out how the journal ended up in the same chest as all that other stuff?"

"I haven't a clue. It's kind of eerie, don't you think?"

"Hey, you know, if you don't mind, I'd like to have our old journal."

Emmy blanched at the suggestion. As much as it pained her to have possession of it again, she also couldn't imagine letting go of it.

"I, um, I want to keep it," she said slowly.

"Oh. Well, could I at least take a look at it sometime?"

"Sure." She breathed a sigh of relief that they wouldn't have to fight over it. "It's pretty funny, you know. Those old pictures, the bad poetry," she said, trying to force a little lightness into the conversation. "What were we thinking?"

"We were kids. We weren't thinking." He smiled, and she relaxed by a degree.

"I'll drop it off at your place later tonight," she said. "I'm not sure where it is among all the boxes."

"No hurry," he said, but his gaze seemed to search her for something, some answer to a question he hadn't asked.

And as they walked back to their respective houses silently, side by side, Emmy could feel the question hanging between them, and she still didn't know what it was.

Or maybe she just didn't *want* to know.

CHAPTER SIXTEEN

The physical wounds and the staph infection began to heal, and those of us who'd made it out of Darfur were visited by chaplains and therapists, all well-meaning people who were supposed to heal the wounds no one could see. They were supposed to help us find solace in God or Carl Jung, and we were supposed to comply. But some part of me didn't want to heal. Healing so soon would have felt like disrespecting all the people I'd seen die. It didn't make sense, but then very little about that time in my life did.

From *Through a Soldier's Eyes*
by Aidan Caldwell

AIDAN'S FINAL WEEK at Promise Lake was uneventful. Once he'd declared that he was leaving the lake and nearly finished with the book, he threw himself into the project wholeheartedly, working night and day to polish it into a final draft.

The work was a welcome distraction from his feelings about leaving Emmy and Max—a welcome distraction from everything, really. A big part of him didn't want to leave the lake, or Emmy and Max, behind, and the rest of him knew he had to.

Aidan looked around the doctor's office and took note of all the little details that were supposed to be soothing and conducive to mental healing. Soft, low lighting, with diffused natural light pouring in through the blinds, a neutral color scheme, big cushy couch and chairs to sit on, no sharp objects…

It worked. He felt relaxed here. It was only his second time visiting Dr. Lydia Cormier at her office rather than her coming to his house. The time before had been a part of his agoraphobia treatment—making the breakthrough of leaving home for a session. This time, he was here for his last session and to say goodbye.

He would be leaving Promise Lake tomorrow, and he was as ready as he ever would be. Which was to say, not very.

Dr. Cormier set the timer for their session and cleared her throat. "So," she said. "How are you feeling today?"

"I just mailed the final draft of my book to my agent, so I'm feeling good."

"Congratulations," she said with a smile. "That must be a huge relief."

"It is."

"We discussed before how the book has been an aid to your recovery from the trauma. Do you see finishing the book as a symbolic way of laying to rest your feelings about your time in Darfur?"

He thought of the roller coaster of emotions he'd experienced yesterday as he read through the final draft from start to finish for the first time, and he nodded slowly. "It brought me full circle," he said. "I could hardly believe I'd actually laid out my whole experience in a coherent story, complete with insights."

"You should be proud of yourself. That's a huge accomplishment. Did any unexpected feelings come up for you upon reading the book yourself?"

"I—I didn't expect to feel so…resolved. Like, putting the manuscript in that package and handing it to the courier was almost like I'd put all the bad feelings in that box and mailed them away, too."

"That's a very healthy way of looking at it."

"When I think of letting go of all the pain, it almost feels disrespectful to the people I saw suffering and dying…disrespectful to the whole tragedy."

"What you're doing is quite the opposite, Aidan. You've written a book that will educate the world about what you experienced, and there is no greater way I can think of to honor those people who've died than to tell their story."

Aidan supposed she was right, but his feeling wasn't rational—it was emotional.

"And keep in mind that if you don't put up some emotional boundaries to protect yourself, as you've been doing in your work with me, you could ultimately be destroyed by your feelings. Destroying your own life isn't respectful to those who've suffered, because it takes away your voice, your ability to help, to spread the word."

Okay, he got the point. He nodded, avoiding her direct gaze.

"Please remember, too, that the emotional boundaries are not a crutch to be looked down upon. They are what allow people in helping professions to survive and cope with what they experience, so that they can go on to assist more people."

"I understand," he said. "I suppose I'm having a bit of trouble letting go of the hard feelings, too because I'll be saying goodbye to Emmy and Max when I leave."

"And that will be difficult for you?"

Dr. Cormier, queen of stating the obvious.

Aidan gave her a look that said "Duh."

"Talk to me about your feelings surrounding saying goodbye to Max and Emmy."

He hated when she did this. But he went along, because so far, Lydia Cormier had done a world of good for him.

"In a way, I'm relieved to be going. I was getting more and more attached to them, and I didn't really want to be. I knew Emmy wasn't into giving me a second chance, and there's no sense getting attached to Max when Emmy doesn't want me in their lives."

"It's difficult not getting attached to people you're fond of."

"Yeah. I'm going to miss that kid."

"Do you feel as if you have any unfinished business there?"

"Of course I do," he blurted. "Emmy is the only woman I've ever really loved, and I think I've fallen in love with her kid, too. How can I *not* have unfinished business when I might not ever even see them again?"

"Have you said all of this to Emmy?"

"It wouldn't matter if I did say it."

Lydia nodded slowly. "Then when you say goodbye to them, you need to imagine it like the feeling you had when you put your manuscript in the courier's hands. You're letting go of your feelings, and they don't have to weigh you down anymore."

Like everything else therapists said, Lydia's advice fell into the category of easier said than done.

"You look skeptical," she said when he didn't respond.

"That's probably because I am."

She smiled. "I want you to see this new problem as a victory of sorts for you. You've done an incredible amount of healing in the past three months. You've gone from living completely isolated, afraid to have contact with anyone and resentful of Max and Emmy's presence, to wishing they were going to be a permanent part of your life."

"Basically, I healed so I could get my heart broken. You're right, that's a reason to celebrate. Let's throw a party."

He knew he was being a sarcastic shit, but he didn't care. It was a good thing this was his last therapy session, because he'd just about had it up to his ears with the psychobabble.

"Do you think, perhaps, that you've developed such strong feelings for them in part because they've played a role in your healing process?"

"My strong feelings for Emmy were already there. And how could I not fall for her kid? He's a part of *her*, goddamn it."

"You're feeling angry right now," she said calmly.

"Sorry." He slouched in his chair and glared out the window.

"Just keep in mind that your healing has come from inside yourself. You don't need Max or Emmy to be happy and whole."

"Look, Lydia, I appreciate your help. You've done wonders for me, but it's time to wrap this up. I think we're done here."

"Okay," she said, careful not to react to his abruptness, though he could tell that below the surface, she was taken aback.

He stood up and they said their polite goodbyes. Then he walked out of the therapy office and into the bright, sunny day in the town of Promise. He paused on the sidewalk in front of the downtown office building, looking left then right before crossing the street to his bike.

He didn't need Lydia anymore, that was for sure. But she was wrong about Max and Emmy. They weren't a part of his healing process, or whatever the hell she wanted to call it. They were a part of the reason he knew he had to go to Africa. Because anywhere on the same continent as them was too close for comfort. Too close to heal from a broken heart.

BY FRIDAY, his last day at the cabin, Aidan realized Max hadn't knocked on his door all week. Emmy must have warned him that Aidan was working, or maybe Max was just avoiding him out of a sense of self-protection. Either way, Aidan felt a sharp stab of sadness when he looked out the window Friday morning and saw Max getting in the car with his mother to leave for the summer day camp he went to every day now.

He had to say goodbye, but... As he watched them, he couldn't will his feet to move. He felt the same scared paralysis as when his agoraphobia had been at its worst, and he simply stood there dumbly staring out the window as they drove away.

He would leave a note for each of them, at least. Setting his one bag of stuff, along with his laptop case, near the front door, he went to the desk and found a notepad and pen there.

To the kid he wrote:

Dear Max,
I hope I'll get to read your next book someday soon. It's been a fun summer getting to know you. You're a great kid. I'll be thinking of you.
Your pirate friend,
Aidan.

He stopped and blinked away the tears in his eyes. He was a damn fool. He'd gone and fallen in love with a grubby little kid who liked to collect rocks and tell stories about ghosts and pirates.

He loved Max, and it ripped another goddamn hole in his chest to have to leave him like this.

And to Emmy, he wrote on a separate piece of paper,

I wish you a good life. The key to the cabin is
under the doormat where I found it.
Ciao,
Aidan.

It was a cop-out, perhaps. But he couldn't write
anything emotional, because he feared if he got started,
he'd say a million things he'd regret later. So he would
say nothing at all.

She knew how he felt. Which was why she'd avoided
him all week.

She knew he'd always loved her and always would.

She knew.

He walked across the property and tucked the notes
into their door, then returned to the cabin, grabbed his
bags, locked the door and loaded the bags into the cargo
carrier on the motorcycle.

He didn't want to be sentimental now. There was
nothing left for him here.

CHAPTER SEVENTEEN

Author's Foreword
Learning to heal from the wounds of my time in Darfur is an ongoing process. This book has been part of the process. Telling my story, and the story of the genocide in Sudan, has been my way of giving a voice to people who couldn't speak to the world for themselves. I cannot adequately speak for them, but I can tell the truth of what I saw, in my own limited way. And I have to thank the people who've helped me heal—Dr. Lydia Cormier, Emmy Van Amsted and Max, who all taught me how to live again.

From *Through a Soldier's Eyes*
by Aidan Caldwell

THE MORNING LIGHT in the cabin felt impossibly sad to Emmy. She looked around the space where Aidan had spent all his days and nights, and she felt for the first time the emptiness he had left behind.

She still held his goodbye note to her in her hand. She'd come straight over after reading it, somehow wanting to see for herself that he was really gone, that this wasn't something she'd imagined.

And also, she realized now, wanting to find some piece of him left behind. Ridiculous and pointless as it was, she searched the cabin, looked in the refrigerator, under the couch, inside the closets, for any little piece of Aidan that might still be there.

But she found nothing. In the desk where he'd kept his computer though, she found an envelope. It sat right in the front of the otherwise empty top drawer, almost as if it had been placed there to be found.

It was addressed to Walter Elliot, with no stamp and no return address. Emmy opened it with shaky hands and began reading.

Dearest Walter,

I'm not sure I'll have the courage to send this letter, so if you do receive it, please know that it was sent after much agonizing.

It was only after I saw your wedding announcement in the mail that I understood the depth of my mistake. I never meant to turn you away, and yet I have. And you are lost to me forever. I will not forget you. But you must know how I feel. I do love you, Walter, and I believe we were meant to be together.

I am a selfish fool for only realizing that now.

I have no one but myself to blame, and I fear I cannot live with the weight of my foolishness.

Emmy stopped reading. Her eyes clouded with tears.

She looked at the envelope again. There was no postmark, and no stamp. The letter had never been mailed. But the date on it was months later than the last one in the pile of letters from Walter, if Emmy remembered correctly.

So their love affair had ended because of Leticia, and she'd regretted it. But she must have known too that sending such a letter as this one would probably make everyone feel worse… Or would it?

Had Walter loved her still, but married someone else? It seemed awfully quick on the heels of his breakup with Leticia that he was sending out a wedding announcement. Emmy supposed in the old days of courting, a quick wedding on the heels of having loved someone else might not have been so unusual.

How did this letter get here, now? Why was it sitting in Aidan's desk, when all the other letters had been stowed away in the chest and buried in the woods?

The hair on the back of Emmy's neck stood up again, as she contemplated the supernatural possibilities. She didn't believe the ghost of Leticia Van Amsted was roaming the property. She did believe Aidan had probably found the letter somewhere in the cabin and left it out for her to find and include with the other letters.

He knew how she'd been interested in Leticia's story, after all.

And this letter… It was the key to the woman's death. Emmy understood now. She'd been heartbroken, and she'd committed suicide. All over the loss of a man.

It seemed tragic, but Emmy was thankful she'd never felt such depths of despair. Probably the only good thing about divorcing when a child was involved was that it kept her focused on what was important. Namely, taking care of Max, regardless of how awful she'd felt at her lowest points.

But as she sat here alone in the cabin that had been Aidan's home for so many months, she could not shake the feeling of loss that was settling more and more firmly in her gut.

She had lost Aidan.

And she understood in a personal way the depths of Leticia's despair. She had not felt it with the end of her marriage, but she could touch that feeling now. She could reach it, feel the shape of it, and almost see its rocky bottom.

Aidan was gone. She'd blown it with him, this one final time, and there would not be another chance for them.

She understood now, too that what she'd been afraid of with Aidan wasn't about any flaw on his part. He was the best man she'd ever known and would probably ever know.

It was about her.

It was about her being afraid of how completely she wanted him. Those feelings went against everything she thought she wanted. She thought she'd wanted independence, never to rely on anyone again, a chance to prove that she was the only person she needed.

But when she thought of how Max would feel when he saw that goodbye note from Aidan, she understood exactly how stupid it was to think it was better not to need anyone.

Of course she needed people. She needed Max. She needed friends. She needed family.

She needed Aidan.

Sure she could take care of herself. Sure she could stand on her own two feet—she'd proven that. But did any of it really matter in the end, when she had a perfectly wonderful man in her life that she could have loved?

That she did love?

She loved Aidan.

She really did. Not in the childish, self-centered, what-can-he-do-for-me way she'd loved him over a decade ago, but in a grown-up kind of way that he deserved to know about.

And she needed to allow herself to feel that love. She wasn't the same person she used to be. Because her grown-up self had fallen in love with Aidan didn't mean she was going to revert to immaturity. It didn't mean that if she allowed herself to feel the big, consuming love she could feel for Aidan, that she was going to flake out and run away like Steven had.

It simply meant that she was capable of loving Aidan the way he deserved to be loved.

The letter she'd been gripping so tightly fell from her hand as she relaxed her hold on it, and she watched it fall to the floor. It landed face up, its ends bending toward her, and she stared at the words on the page without seeing them. The delicate, spidery handwriting formed meaningless designs on the page.

Someone's heart dwelled in those words that seemed so meaningless if she wasn't looking at them the right way.

It was all about perspective.

Emmy had just let her last chance with the best guy she'd ever known slip through her fingers, and he'd never know how she felt unless she told him.

Which she hadn't. Just like Leticia, she was choosing to stay silent when speaking up might make a difference.

Just like Leticia, who'd died, essentially, from her inability to follow her heart. If she'd sent the letter, maybe the effort of speaking up would have saved her. Maybe she wouldn't have ended up with Walter, but maybe she'd have lived on to find some other chance at love.

Emmy felt tears well in her eyes, then overflow onto her cheeks. She had to tell Aidan how she felt. Maybe it wouldn't change anything, and maybe her chance with him was really gone for good, but at least she'd know she had tried. She'd have given it one more shot.

She had to go now, before he was on a plane, then two continents and an ocean away. She had to find him. But who would know where he was?

Her father.

The thought of calling Robert Van Amsted stopped Emmy cold. She couldn't do that.

She owed it to Aidan, to herself, to get over the bitterness at her father at least long enough to pick up the phone and call.

Before she could change her mind, Emmy rose and

hurried to her house. In her office, she dug around in her desk until she found her address book, and she looked up her father's number, which she called so rarely she didn't know it by heart.

Then she picked up her phone and dialed. When her father answered, his voice resonated deep in her belly, in places where she'd learned to respond to him as a child, when he was the most important man in her world and could do anything, when she'd viewed him with adoration and awe.

She squeezed her eyes tight, then forced herself to say, "Hi Dad. It's me, Emmy."

"Emmy, my girl. What a nice surprise. How's life out there at Promise Lake?"

It was just like her father to pretend it was totally normal for her to be calling, to start talking to her as if there were no bad feelings and it was perfectly normal for a father and daughter to exchange only small-talk conversations on major holidays. Maybe for him, it *was* normal. And at that moment, Emmy was grateful for his inability to understand the depths of her feelings.

"It's good," she said. "I've got my house nearly finished, and we're happy here."

"I'm glad to hear it. You owe me some pictures of that boy of yours. I'm tired of getting them only whenever your mother remembers to send them to me."

"Sorry, Dad," she said. "Maybe you could come out for a visit soon. Max would like to see you," she said before she could change her mind.

It wasn't until that moment that she understood how

selfish and unfair she was being to keep Max from having a relationship with his grandfather. No matter what Emmy felt about her father's indiscretions, it shouldn't prevent Max from knowing him, or vice versa.

And maybe it shouldn't have prevented Emmy from knowing her father either. She didn't really know him anymore. Maybe he'd changed in the years they'd been apart. And maybe he hadn't, but she was ready to find out. Maybe even ready not to let his flaws bother her—at least not so much that she had to shut him out of her life.

"I've been thinking that myself now that the cabin's empty again. You sure you won't mind me being there?"

"It's fine. We'd like to see you."

"I'd like to see you, too."

"I'm calling because I was wondering if you know when or where Aidan's flying back to Africa."

She heard papers shuffling in the background on her dad's end. "I do, actually."

She braced herself for him to ask why she wanted to know. She didn't want to have to explain to her father her reasons for wanting to find Aidan now.

But he didn't ask, thank goodness. "I've got his flight information right here," he said finally.

He read the flight number and airline, leaving San Francisco International at 1:15 p.m. Emmy glanced at the clock. If she left now, and didn't hit any traffic, she might be able to make it to the airport before his flight took off.

"Does he have a cell phone number?" she asked.

"Nope, not that I know of."

She had to try to catch him at the airport.

"Thanks, Dad," she said. "I've got to run, but I hope you do make it out here soon."

When she hung up, Emmy sprang into action, grabbing her shoes and purse and hurrying out the door. She'd have to call around on the way to find someone who could pick Max up from school and keep him for the evening.

It was only when she'd climbed into the car that she noticed she was still wearing her old, stained yoga pants and T-shirt that she'd put on intending to paint the walls today, but there wasn't time to change clothes now, so she started the car and pulled out of the driveway.

And as she headed toward San Francisco, she felt as if she were leaving her old self behind on the way to becoming someone new, shrugging off the ties that bound her to the past, headed toward the woman she was meant to be and the life she was meant to live.

AIDAN HATED airport lines as much as anyone, but the one he was standing in now felt especially torturous. Thanks to traffic in the Marina district where he'd left his motorcycle in a friend's garage, he was late for his flight, which was leaving in exactly twenty-five minutes. But this was of no concern to the airport security personnel whose job it was to make sure he didn't smuggle any six-ounce tubes of toothpaste onto the plane.

And thanks to a suspicious-looking bottle of liquid he had in his overnight bag that was just mouthwash, he was now stuck standing in the line of people who were waiting to be given the extra-thorough checking out.

"Excuse me," he said to the large, surly-looking man who was doing an item-by-item inspection of the overnight pack of the woman standing in front of him. "I'm late for my flight. Is there any way you could hurry me through here?"

"I'll be right with you," the man, whose nametag read Sonny, said in the most leisurely tone Aidan had ever heard spoken aloud.

His temper flared, but he said nothing. He had a feeling pissing off Sonny was only going to make him move even more slowly. The guard sorted through the woman's clothes, shoes and toiletries, checked all the pockets of the bag, and then—finally—gave her the go-ahead to move on.

He was about to check Aidan's backpack when a familiar voice called out from the other side of the security barrier.

"Aidan!"

He looked over to see Emmy standing there, and for a moment he couldn't make sense of it. How had Emmy gotten here? She was supposed to be at Promise Lake. She couldn't be here right now.

But she was.

"Okay, sir, you can move on through," the security guard said to him.

His plane was leaving in twenty minutes.

"I need to talk to that lady over there. Could she come through for just a minute?"

"Only passengers are allowed on this side," the guard said as if he was repeating a refrain he'd already stated a thousand times that day.

Aidan glanced toward the gate where his plane was boarding, then he looked back toward Emmy.

"I need to talk to you. Please!" she called out.

Her tone told him everything he needed to know about whether he should risk missing his flight. He muttered a curse, slung his backpack over his shoulder and headed toward the exit of the security area.

Screw it. Emmy was looking at him so desperately, his stomach was coiling tight with fear that something bad had happened. What if Max was hurt? The thought made him pick up his pace until he was nearly running by the time he reached her.

"What is it? What are you doing here?" he asked, his mind still trying to wrap around the simple fact that she was there at the airport.

Emmy looked as if she was about to burst into tears. She squeezed her eyes shut tight for a moment, then opened them and took a deep breath.

"Oh my God, I made it. I—I thought I'd miss you."

"You almost did. I'm about to miss my flight."

"I'm sorry. I just… Aidan, I was so wrong. I was wrong."

"What are you talking about?"

"You. And me. I was wrong about us. I was afraid."

"Afraid of what?"

"Of being with you."

"Oh."

"But I do want to be with you."

"You drove all this way to tell me that?"

He looked her up and down for the first time and saw that she was wearing her old painting clothes. Like she'd dropped what she was doing and come here in a big hurry. She would have had to, to make it here before his flight left.

None of it was making any sense.

"No," she said, shaking her head hard. "I drove all this way to tell you I love you and I want to do whatever it takes to have you in my life."

"What?"

Her words didn't register at first.

She...loved...him? "I love you, Aidan. I do. And I want you in my life, not in Africa. Please, if there's any way you can not go, if there's any way you can stay— please don't go."

Nothing she was saying made any damn sense. Except, the look in Emmy's eyes told him she was distraught. She really didn't want him to leave. That much was clear. But driving all this way and keeping him from his flight to tell him she loved him...

It couldn't mean what he hoped it meant. He didn't dare let his heart hope.

"I—I have to go," he said, shaking his head.

She looked stricken. "Please, Aidan. I know I don't deserve a second chance, but I realized something today. I can't let you walk out of my life again without at least letting you know how I feel. So hear me, and if you still want to leave, I'll understand. I love you, and I want us to be together. Really together. I want you to be a part of my life, and Max's life, and—"

He got it now. He didn't need her to keep explaining. Aidan dropped his bag on the floor and closed the distance between them. He took her in his arms and kissed her then, letting his whole self relax into the idea that she really meant what she said.

She was his, if he wanted her to be. And he did.

"Let's go home," he said against her mouth as they broke the kiss.

Emmy smiled. "But, what about your flight?"

He laughed. "I love you, too, Emmy. I don't give a damn about the flight. My friend will understand that I can't come to Africa after all."

"You can't?"

"No, not now."

"What will you do then?"

Aidan shrugged. "I've been thinking about writing another book, actually. A novel this time. I'm done with nonfiction."

"What kind of novel?"

"An epic love story, perhaps," he said, only half-joking.

"I know a great cabin where you could work," she said as they began walking toward the airport exit.

"I think I'm going to need a lot of inspiration in the form of, you know, romance."

"Oh, right. I think I can help you out with that," she said.

He knew she would. She'd already taught him everything he needed to know about love.

* * * * *

'I'VE FOUND HER.'

Max froze.

It was what he'd been waiting for since June, but now—now he was almost afraid to voice the question. His heart stalling, he leaned slowly back in his chair and scoured the investigator's face for clues. 'Where?' he asked, and his voice sounded rough and unused, like a rusty hinge.

'In Suffolk. She's living in a cottage.'

Living. His heart crashed back to life, and he sucked in a long, slow breath. All these months he'd feared—

'Is she well?'

'Yes, she's well.'

He had to force himself to ask the next question. 'Alone?'

The man paused. 'No. The cottage belongs to a man called John Blake. He's working away at the moment, but he comes and goes.'

God. He felt sick. So sick he hardly registered the next few words, but then gradually they sank in. 'She's got *what?*'

'Babies. Twin girls. They're eight months old.'

'Eight—?' he echoed under his breath. 'They must be his.'

He was thinking out loud, but the P.I. heard and corrected him.

'Apparently not. I gather they're hers. She's been there since mid-January last year, and they were born during the summer—June, the woman in the post office thought. She was more than helpful. I think there's been a certain amount of speculation about their relationship.'

He'd just bet there had. God, he was going to kill her. Or Blake. Maybe both of them.

'Of course, looking at the dates, she was presumably pregnant when she left you, so they could be yours, or she could have been having an affair with this Blake character before...'

He glared at the unfortunate P.I. 'Just stick to your job. I can do the math,' he snapped, swallowing the unpalatable possibility that she'd been unfaithful to him before she'd left. 'Where is she? I want the address.'

'It's all in here,' the man said, sliding a large envelope across the desk to him. 'With my invoice.'

'I'll get it seen to. Thank you.'

'If there's anything else you need, Mr Gallagher, any further information—'

'I'll be in touch.'

'The woman in the post office told me Blake was away at the moment, if that helps,' he added quietly, and opened the door.

Max stared down at the envelope, hardly daring to open it, but when the door clicked softly shut behind the P.I., he eased up the flap, tipped it and felt his breath jam in his throat as the photos spilled out over the desk.

Oh, lord, she looked gorgeous. Different, though. It took him a moment to recognise her, because she'd grown her hair, and it was tied back in a ponytail, making her look younger and somehow freer. The blond highlights were gone, and it was back to its natural soft golden-brown, with a little curl in the end of the ponytail that he wanted to thread his finger through and tug, just gently, to draw her back to him.

Crazy. She'd put on a little weight, but it suited her. She looked well and happy and beautiful, but oddly, considering how desperate he'd been for news of her for the past year—one year, three weeks and two days, to be exact—it wasn't only Julia who held his attention after the initial shock. It was the babies sitting side by side in a supermarket trolley. Two identical and absolutely beautiful little girls.

* * * * *

When Max Gallagher hires a P.I. to find his estranged wife, Julia, he discovers she's not alone— she has twin baby girls, and they might be his. Now workaholic Max has just two weeks to prove that he can be a wonderful husband and father to the family he wants to treasure.

Look for TWO LITTLE MIRACLES by
Caroline Anderson,
available February 2009 from Harlequin Romance®.

HARLEQUIN® Romance®

This February the Harlequin® Romance series
will feature six Diamond Brides stories featuring
diamond proposals and gorgeous grooms.

Share your dream wedding proposal and you could WIN!

The most romantic entry will win a diamond
necklace and will inspire a proposal in one of
our upcoming Diamond Grooms books in 2010.

In 100 words or less, tell us the most romantic
way that you dream of being proposed to.

For more information, and to enter
the Diamond Brides Proposal contest, please visit
www.DiamondBridesProposal.com

Or mail your entry to us at:
IN THE U.S.: 3010 Walden Ave., P.O. Box 9069, Buffalo, NY 14269-9069
IN CANADA: 225 Duncan Mill Road, Don Mills, ON M3B 3K9

REQUEST YOUR FREE BOOKS!

2 FREE NOVELS PLUS 2 FREE GIFTS!

HARLEQUIN®

Super Romance®

Exciting, emotional, unexpected!

COMING NEXT MONTH

#1542 THE STORY BETWEEN THEM • Molly O'Keefe
Jennifer Stern has left journalism to focus on life with her son. Then
Ian Greer—son of a former president—picks her to tell the true story of
his family, and it's a scoop she can't resist. But could her attraction to Ian
jeopardize the piece?

#1543 A COWBOY'S REDEMPTION • Jeannie Watt
Home on the Ranch
Kira Jennings just wants access across Jason Ross's land so she can subdivide
her property and sell it off...and save face with her CEO, aka grandfather.
Sure, there's bad blood between Jason and her brother. She didn't realize
exactly *how* bad. Until now.

#1544 THE HERO'S SIN • Darlene Gardner
Return to Indigo Springs
Good thing Sarah Brenneman doesn't judge a book by its cover. Otherwise she'd
believe what the town's gossips say about Michael Donahue. Instead, she's
impressed by his heroics. Still, can she believe what her heart is telling her
about Michael, or could those rumors end their romance before it even begins?

#1545 A KID TO THE RESCUE • Susan Gable
Suddenly a Parent
Shannon Vanderhoff knows that everybody and everything are temporary
gifts. So when she becomes guardian of her six-year-old, traumatized nephew,
how can she give him the help he needs without falling for him? It takes
Greg Hawkins's art therapy class to turn the child around...and it takes a kid
to create this loving family.

#1546 THE THINGS WE DO FOR LOVE • Margot Early
The man Mary Anne Drew loves is marrying someone else. So she buys a love
potion to win him back. Too bad the wrong man drinks it! Graham Corbett has
never shown any interest in Mary Anne before. Could the potion really work?
Or was she looking for love in the wrong place all along?

#1547 WHAT FAMILY MEANS • Geri Krotow
Everlasting Love
Debra and Will Bradley wanted their kids to know that family means
everything. Through hard and joyous times, Debra and Will have never
questioned that. Now Angie, their daughter, is pregnant—and separated.
Award-winning author Geri Krotow tells a memorable story of how marriage
and family define our lives.

HSRCNMBPA0109